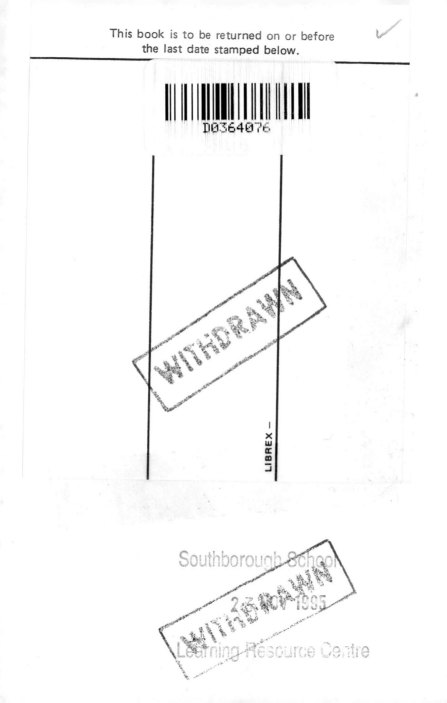

THE NEW WINDMILL BOOK OF
SHORT STORIES
BY WOMEN

EDITED BY MIKE HAMLIN,
CHRISTINE HALL AND JANE BROWNE

Heinemann
New Windmills

Heinemann Educational
a division of
Heinemann Publishers (Oxford) Ltd
Halley Court, Jordan Hill, Oxford OX2 8EJ
OXFORD LONDON EDINBURGH
MADRID ATHENS BOLOGNA PARIS
MELBOURNE SYDNEY AUCKLAND SINGAPORE TOKYO
IBADAN NAIROBI HARARE GABARONE
PORTSMOUTH NH (USA)

First published in the New Windmill Series 1995

95 96 97 98 99 10 9 8 7 6 5 4 3 2 1

ISBN 0 435 12432 3

British Library Cataloguing in Publication Data
for this title is available from the British Library

Contents

Introduction

Short Stories by Women is the third in a series of New Windmill short story collections specifically designed to broaden the range of writing available to younger readers. *Nineteenth Century Short Stories* introduced a rich variety of nineteenth-century writing and *Classic Short Stories* presented a diverse collection of accessible stories by well-known authors.

This third volume brings the best of women's writing to a younger audience. Schools often feel that their current book stock does not fully represent the strength of women's writing and many will welcome the opportunity to introduce students to the powerful writers represented in this collection.

English in the National Curriculum insists that, 'Pupils should be given opportunities to read a wide variety of literature and to respond to the substance and style of texts.' They should also 'read texts from other cultures and traditions that represent their distinctive voices and forms.'

The nineteen stories in this collection have all been chosen for their power and accessibility in the classroom. But in reading and enjoying these stories pupils will experience a fascinating range of writing. There are stories here from Australia, New Zealand, the United States, Canada, South Africa and India, as well as Britain. The stories also span a period of time from Kate Chopin writing in the nineteenth century, through to the very best of contemporary authors.

The language and traditions of different cultures are represented in the stories, from the island life of Barbados explored by Paule Marshall, to Anita Desai's story 'Games at Twilight' set in India.

To start you thinking, we have grouped the stories loosely according to theme. This suggests one way of making comparisons and should help you to think about other possible ways of understanding the stories. However, each story stands on its own with many potential links and contrasts. Readers will find in this selection a variety of ways of telling stories with many associated themes to explore.

We have provided specific background information on each author to help in contextualising the stories and also to give an indication of other titles pupils might like to explore for their own wider reading. Some of these authors such as Anita Desai, Penelope Lively and Jane Gardam have written explicitly for children whilst others are writing for a more adult audience.

And finally – do women writers have a particular way of seeing of the world? Does their experience as women mean that they tend to tackle certain themes in preference to others? The best way of answering these questions is to read the stories in this volume for yourself!

Katherine Mansfield

Katherine Mansfield Beauchamp was born in Wellington, New Zealand in 1888, the third daughter in a family of four girls and one boy. She spent her early years in Karori, near Wellington and attended the local county school. In 1903, at the age of fifteen, Katherine Mansfield was sent to Queen's College, the first institution to be created in England for the higher education of women. Here she was encouraged to read widely, and she also became an accomplished cello player.

Three years later she returned to New Zealand but hated it, feeling herself cut off from life, and writing of the 'narrow, sodden, mean, draggled houses'. Her return to England in July 1908 saw her continuing to write, but without a market for her sort of writing. She was not interested in stories with a plot and happy endings, but wanted to write about the things she saw around her. Her aim was, 'to intensify the small things so that truly everything was significant'.

The year of 1909 proved an unhappy and turbulent one for Katherine Mansfield. Disappointed with one love affair she made a rapid decision to marry George Bowden, but left him after a few days. She went to Woerishofen, a Bavarian spa town, where she had a stillbirth. Her time in Bavaria formed the basis for her first collection of stories *In A German Pension* (1911).

On her return to England, Katherine Mansfield met and later married John Middleton Murry, a critic and magazine editor who published her writing in magazines. The publication of *Bliss and Other Stories* (1910) brought widespread recognition. Despite increasing ill-health she continued writing, publishing *The Garden Party and Other Stories* (1922) and her *Journal* which was published after her death. She died in 1923 when she was only 34 years old.

The story 'Sixpence', concerns itself with parents' uncertainties about the best way to bring up their children.

Sixpence

Katherine Mansfield

Children are unaccountable little creatures. Why should a small boy like Dicky, good as gold as a rule, sensitive, affectionate, obedient, and marvellously sensible for his age, have moods when, without the slightest warning, he suddenly went 'mad dog,' as his sisters called it, and there was no doing anything with him?

'Dicky, come here! Come here, sir, at once! Do you hear your mother calling you? Dicky!'

But Dicky wouldn't come. Oh, he heard right enough. A clear, ringing little laugh was his only reply. And away he flew; hiding, running through the uncut hay on the lawn, dashing past the woodshed, making a rush for the kitchen garden, and there dodging, peering at his mother from behind the mossy apple trunks, and leaping up and down like a wild Indian.

It had begun at tea-time. While Dicky's mother and Mrs Spears, who was spending the afternoon with her, were quietly sitting over their sewing in the drawing room, this, according to the servant girl, was what had happened at the children's tea. They were eating their first bread and butter as nicely and quietly as you please, and the servant girl had just poured out the milk and water, when Dicky had suddenly seized the bread plate, put it upside down on his head, and clutched the bread knife.

'Look at me!' he shouted.

His startled sisters looked, and before the servant girl could get there, the bread plate wobbled, slid, flew to the floor, and broke into shivers. At this awful point the little girls lifted up their voices and shrieked their loudest.

'Mother, come and look what he's done!'

'Dicky's broke a great big plate!'

'Come and stop him, mother!'

You can imagine how mother came flying. But she was too late. Dicky had leapt out of his chair, run through the french windows on to the veranda, and, well – there she stood – popping her thimble on and off, helpless. What could she do? She couldn't chase after the child. She couldn't stalk Dicky among the apples and damsons. That would be too undignified. It was more than annoying, it was exasperating. Especially as Mrs Spears, Mrs Spears of all people, whose two boys were so exemplary, was waiting for her in the drawing-room.

'Very well, Dicky,' she cried, 'I shall have to think of some way of punishing you.'

'I don't care,' sounded the high little voice, and again there came that ringing laugh. The child was quite beside himself . . .

'Oh, Mrs Spears, I don't know how to apologise for leaving you by yourself like this.'

'It's quite all right, Mrs Bendall,' said Mrs Spears, in her soft, sugary voice, and raising her eyebrows in the way she had. She seemed to smile to herself as she stroked the gathers. 'These little things will happen from time to time. I only hope it was nothing serious.'

'It was Dicky,' said Mrs Bendall, looking rather helplessly for her only fine needle. And she explained the whole affair to Mrs Spears. 'And the worst of it is, I don't know how to cure him. Nothing when he's in that mood seems to have the slightest effect on him.'

Mrs Spears opened her pale eyes. 'Not even a whipping?' said she.

But Mrs Bendall, threading her needle, pursed up her lips. 'We never have whipped the children,' she said. 'The girls never seem to have needed it. And Dicky is such a baby, and the only boy. Somehow . . .'

'Oh, my dear,' said Mrs Spears, and she laid her sewing down. 'I don't wonder Dicky has these little outbreaks. You don't mind me saying so? But I'm sure you make a great mistake in trying to bring up children without whipping them. Nothing really takes its place. And I speak from experience, my dear. I used to try gentler measures' – Mrs Spears drew in her breath with a little hissing sound –

'soaping the boys' tongues, for instance, with yellow soap, or making them stand on the table for the whole of Saturday afternoon. But no, believe me,' said Mrs Spears, 'there is nothing, there is nothing like handing them over to their father.'

Mrs Bendall in her heart of hearts was dreadfully shocked to hear of that yellow soap. But Mrs Spears seemed to take it so much for granted, that she did too.

'Their father,' she said. 'Then you don't whip them yourself?'

'Never.' Mrs Spears seemed quite shocked at the idea. 'I don't think it's the mother's place to whip the children. It's the duty of the father. And, besides, he impresses them so much more.'

'Yes, I can imagine that,' said Mrs Bendall faintly.

'Now my two boys,' Mrs Spears smiled kindly, encouragingly, at Mrs Bendall, 'would behave just like Dicky if they were not afraid to. As it is . . .'

'Oh, your boys are perfect little models,' cried Mrs Bendall.

They were. Quieter, better-behaved little boys, in the presence of grown-ups, could not be found. In fact, Mrs Spears' callers often made the remark that you never would have known that there was a child in the house. There wasn't – very often.

In the front hall, under a large picture of fat, cheery old monks fishing by the riverside, there was a thick, dark horse-whip that had belonged to Mr Spears' father. And for some reason the boys preferred to play out of sight of this, behind the dog-kennel or in the tool-house, or round about the dustbin.

'It's such a mistake,' sighed Mrs Spears, breathing softly, as she folded her work, 'to be weak with children when they are little. It's such a sad mistake, and one so easy to make. It's so unfair to the child. That is what one has to remember. Now Dicky's little escapade this afternoon seemed to me as though he'd done it on purpose. It was the child's way of showing you that he needed a whipping.'

'Do you really think so?' Mrs Bendall was a weak little thing, and this impressed her very much.

'I do; I feel sure of it. And a sharp reminder now and

then,' cried Mrs Spears in quite a professional manner, 'administered by the father, will save you so much trouble in the future. Believe me, my dear.' She put her dry, cold hand over Mrs Bendall's.

'I shall speak to Edward the moment he comes in,' said Dicky's mother firmly.

The children had gone to bed before the garden gate banged, and Dicky's father staggered up the steep concrete steps carrying his bicycle. It had been a bad day at the office. He was hot, dusty, tired out.

But by this time, Mrs Bendall had become quite excited over the new plan, and she opened the door to him herself.

'Oh, Edward, I'm so thankful you have come home,' she cried.

'Why, what's happened?' Edward lowered the bicycle and took off his hat. A red angry pucker showed where the brim had pressed. 'What's up?'

'Come – come into the drawing-room,' said Mrs Bendall, speaking very fast. 'I simply can't tell you how naughty Dicky has been. You have no idea – you can't have at the office all day – how a child of that age can behave. He's been simply dreadful. I have no control over him – none. I've tried everything, Edward, but it's all no use. The only thing to do,' she finished breathlessly, 'is to whip him – is for you to whip him, Edward.'

In the corner of the drawing-room there was a what-not, and on the top shelf stood a brown china bear with a painted tongue. It seemed in the shadow to be grinning at Dicky's father, to be saying, 'Hooray, this is what you've come home to!'

'But why on earth should I start whipping him?' said Edward, staring at the bear. 'We've never done it before.'

'Because,' said his wife, 'don't you see, it's the only thing to do. I can't control the child . . .' Her words flew from her lips. They beat round him, beat round his tired head. 'We can't possibly afford a nurse. The servant girl has more than enough to do. And his naughtiness is beyond words. You don't understand, Edward; you can't, you're at the office all day.'

The bear poked out his tongue. The scolding voice went on. Edward sank into a chair.

'What am I to beat him with?' he said weakly.

'Your slipper, of course,' said his wife. And she knelt down to untie his dusty shoes.

'Oh, Edward,' she wailed, 'you've still got your cycling clips on in the drawing-room. No, really – '

'Here, that's enough.' Edward nearly pushed her away. 'Give me that slipper.' He went up the stairs. He felt like a man in a dark net. And now he wanted to beat Dicky. Yes, damn it, he wanted to beat something. My God, what a life! The dust was still in his hot eyes, his arms felt heavy.

He pushed open the door of Dicky's slip of a room. Dicky was standing in the middle of the floor in his night-shirt. At the sight of him Edward's heart gave a warm throb of rage.

'Well, Dicky, you know what I've come for,' said Edward.

Dicky made no reply.

'I've come to give you a whipping.'

No answer.

'Lift up your night-shirt.'

At that Dicky looked up. He flushed a deep pink. 'Must I?' he whispered.

'Come on, now. Be quick about it,' said Edward, and, grasping the slipper, he gave Dicky three hard slaps.

'There, that'll teach you to behave properly to your mother.'

Dicky stood there, hanging his head.

'Look sharp and get into bed,' said his father.

Still he did not move. But a shaking voice said, 'I've not done my teeth yet, Daddy.'

'Eh, what's that?'

Dicky looked up. His lips were quivering, but his eyes were dry. He hadn't made a sound or shed a tear. Only he swallowed and said huskily, 'I haven't done my teeth, Daddy.'

But at the sight of that little face Edward turned, and, not knowing what he was doing, he bolted from the room, down the stairs, and out into the garden. Good God! What had he done? He strode along and hid in the shadow of the pear tree by the hedge. Whipped Dicky – whipped his little man with a slipper – and what the devil for? He didn't even know. Suddenly he barged into his room – and there was the little chap in his night-shirt. Dicky's father groaned and held on to the hedge. And he didn't cry. Never a tear. If only he'd cried or got angry. But that 'Daddy'! And again he heard the quivering whisper. Forgiving like that without a word. But he'd never forgive himself – never. Coward! Fool! Brute! And suddenly he remembered the time when Dicky had fallen off his knee and sprained his wrist while they were playing together. He hadn't cried then, either. And that was the little hero he had just whipped.

Something's got to be done about this, thought Edward. He strode back to the house, up the stairs, into Dicky's room. The little boy was lying in bed. In the half-light his dark head, with the square fringe, showed plain against the pale pillow. He was lying quite still, and even now he wasn't crying. Edward shut the door and leaned against it. What he wanted to do was to kneel down by Dicky's bed and cry himself and beg to be forgiven. But, of course, one can't do that sort of thing. He felt awkward, and his heart was wrung.

'Not asleep yet, Dicky?' he said lightly.

'No, Daddy.'

Edward came over and sat on his boy's bed, and Dicky looked at him through his long lashes.

'Nothing the matter, little chap, is there?' said Edward, half whispering.

'No-o, Daddy,' came from Dicky.

Edward put out his hand, and carefully he took Dicky's hot little paw.

'You – you mustn't think any more of what happened just now, little man,' he said huskily. 'See? That's all over now. That's forgotten. That's never going to happen again. See?'

'Yes, Daddy.'

'So the thing to do now is to buck up, little chap,' said Edward, 'and to smile.' And he tried himself an extraordinary trembling apology for a smile. 'To forget all about it – to – eh? Little man . . . Old boy. . . .'

Dicky lay as before. This was terrible. Dicky's father sprang up and went over to the window. It was nearly dark in the garden. The servant girl had run out, and she was snatching, twitching some white clothes off the bushes and piling them over her arm. But in the boundless sky the evening star shone, and a big gum tree, black against the pale glow, moved its long leaves softly. All this he saw, while he felt in his trouser pocket for his money. Bringing it out, he chose a new sixpence and went back to Dicky.

'Here you are, little chap. Buy yourself something,' said Edward softly, laying the sixpence on Dicky's pillow.

But could even that – could even a whole sixpence – blot out what had been? (1921)

Grace Paley

Grace Paley was born in New York in 1922, the child of Jewish parents who had only recently emigrated from Russia. They lived in one of the poorer districts of Manhattan; her mother worked in a number of low paid textile jobs, her father studied hard to become a doctor.

The young Grace Paley grew up amongst the vivid life of immigrant New York, a child of many cultures with her father teaching her Yiddish and Russian and the everyday people around her speaking a mixture of accents, dialects and languages.

Paley's main education came from the streets, she had few formal qualifications and failed to complete her course at college. She married early and had two children, a son and a daughter. Only in her middle thirties, with her children relatively independent, did Paley begin to write. She wrote short, often *very* short, stories which were published in a variety of New York literary magazines. To date, three collections of her stories have been published: *The Little Disturbances of Man* (1959), *Enormous Changes at the Last Minute* (1974) and *Later the Same Day* (1985).

Paley has never published a novel and when questioned on this replied, 'Art is too long and life is too short. There is a lot more to do in life than just writing.' A lot of her non-writing life has been given over to political activity, and as a pacifist she was active in both the movement to end the war in Vietnam and in the campaign for nuclear disarmament.

Something of her New York cosmopolitan surroundings and her concern for basic human liberties is reflected in the story chosen here, 'Anxiety'. The young fathers collecting their children from school are very different from the fathers of Grace Paley's generation, but the older woman looking on is still anxious for their futures and she is not afraid to say so.

Anxiety

Grace Paley

The young fathers are waiting outside the school. What curly heads! Such graceful brown mustaches. They're sitting on their haunches eating pizza and exchanging information. They're waiting for the 3 p.m. bell. It's springtime, the season of first looking out the window. I have a window box of greenhouse marigolds. The young fathers can be seen through the ferny leaves.

The bell rings. The children fall out of school, tumbling through the open door. One of the fathers sees his child. A small girl. Is she Chinese? A little. Up u-u-p, he says, and hoists her to his shoulders. U-u-p, says the second father, and hoists his little boy. The little boy sits on top of his father's head for a couple of seconds before sliding to his shoulders. Very funny, says the father.

They start off down the street, right under and past my window. The two children are still laughing. They try to whisper a secret. The fathers haven't finished their conversation. The frailer father is uncomfortable; his little girl wiggles too much.

Stop it this minute, he says.

Oink oink, says the little girl.

What'd you say?

Oink oink, she says.

The young father says What! three times. Then he seizes the child, raises her high above his head, and sets her hard on her feet.

What'd I do so bad, she says, rubbing her ankle.

Just hold my hand, screams the frail and angry father.

I lean far out the window. Stop! Stop! I cry.

The young father turns, shading his eyes, but sees.

What? he says. His friend says, Hey? Who's that? He probably thinks I'm a family friend, a teacher maybe.

Who're you? he says.

I move the pots of marigold aside. Then I'm able to lean on my elbow way out into unshadowed visibility. Once, not too long ago, the tenements were speckled with women like me in every third window up to the fifth story, calling the children from play to receive orders and instruction. This memory enables me to say strictly, Young man, I am an older person who feels free because of that to ask questions and give advice.

Oh? he says, laughs with a little embarrassment, says to his friend, Shoot if you will that old gray head. But he's joking, I know, because he has established himself, legs apart, hands behind his back, his neck arched to see and hear me out.

How old are you? I call. About thirty or so?

Thirty-three.

First I want to say you're about a generation ahead of your father in your attitude and behavior toward your child.

Really? Well? Anything else, ma'am.

Son, I said, leaning another two, three dangerous inches toward him. Son, I must tell you that madmen intend to destroy this beautifully made planet. That the murder of our children by these men has got to become a terror and a sorrow to you, and starting now, it had better interfere with any daily pleasure.

Speech speech, he called.

I waited a minute, but he continued to look up. So, I said, I can tell by your general appearance and loping walk that you agree with me.

I do, he said, winking at his friend; but turning a serious face to mine, he said again, Yes, yes, I do.

Well then, why did you become angry at that little girl whose future is like a film which suddenly cuts to white. Why did you nearly slam this little doomed person to the ground in your uncontrollable anger.

Let's not go too far, said the young father. She *was* jumping around on my poor back and hollering oink oink.

When were you angriest – when she wiggled and jumped or when she said oink?

He scratched his wonderful head of dark well-cut hair. I guess when she said oink.

Have you ever said oink oink? Think carefully. Years ago, perhaps?

No. Well maybe. Maybe.

Whom did you refer to in this way?

He laughed. He called to his friend, Hey Ken, this old person's got something. The cops. In a demonstration. Oink oink, he said, remembering, laughing.

The little girl smiled and said, Oink oink.

Shut up, he said.

What do you deduce from this?

That I was angry at Rosie because she was dealing with me as though I was a figure of authority, and it's not my thing, never has been, never will be.

I could see his happiness, his nice grin, as he remembered this.

So, I continued, since those children are such lovely examples of what may well be the last generation of humankind, why don't you start all over again, right from the school door, as though none of this had ever happened.

Thank you, said the young father. Thank you. It would be nice to be a horse, he said, grabbing little Rosie's hand. Come on Rosie, let's go. I don't have all day.

U-up, says the first father. U-up, says the second.

Giddap, shout the children, and the fathers yell neigh neigh, as horses do. The children kick their fathers' horse-chests, screaming giddap giddap, and they gallop wildly westward.

I lean way out to cry once more, Be careful! Stop! But they've gone too far. Oh, anyone would love to be a fierce fast horse carrying a beloved beautiful rider, but they are galloping toward one of the most dangerous street corners in the world. And they may live beyond that trisection across other dangerous avenues.

So I must shut the window after patting the April-cooled marigolds with their rusty smell of summer. Then I sit in the nice light and wonder how to make sure that they gallop safely home through the airy scary dreams of scientists and the bulky dreams of automakers. I wish I could see just how they sit down at their kitchen tables for a healthy snack (orange juice or milk and cookies) before going out into the new spring afternoon to play.

Nadine Gordimer

Nadine Gordimer was born in 1923 in Springs, near Johannesburg in South Africa. She was educated at a convent school until, at the age of ten, she was diagnosed as having a heart complaint. She was then educated at home by tutors until the age of 15. Her rather solitary life led her to begin writing seriously at the age of nine; her first short story was published when she was fifteen. She was barred from taking a university degree because of her lack of formal education.

Nadine Gordimer's first novel, *The Lying Days*, was published in 1953. This partly autobiographical novel won her widespread respect, and was the beginning of a glittering literary career. Gordimer has won many awards, honorary degrees and prizes for her novels and short stories; in 1991 she was awarded the Nobel Prize for Literature. She has been a fierce opponent of apartheid in her writing, as a result of which some of her novels, such as *Burger's Daughter* (published in 1979), were banned in South Africa. Since the change of government in South Africa, Gordimer has continued to write about the difficulties its people face.

'Once Upon a Time' is a fable from a collection of stories called *Jump*, first published in Britain in 1991. The author's own introduction, which we have included with the story, explains the context in which it was written.

Once Upon a Time

Nadine Gordimer

Someone has written to ask me to contribute to an anthology of stories for children. I reply that I don't write children's stories; and he writes back that at a recent congress/book fair/seminar a certain novelist said every writer ought to write at least one story for children. I think of sending a postcard saying I don't accept that I 'ought' to write anything.

And then last night I woke up – or rather was wakened without knowing what had roused me.

A voice in the echo-chamber of the subconscious?

A sound.

A creaking of the kind made by the weight carried by one foot after another along a wooden floor. I listened. I felt the apertures of my ears distend with concentration. Again: the creaking. I was waiting for it; waiting to hear if it indicated that feet were moving from room to room, coming up the passage – to my door. I have no burglar bars, no gun under the pillow, but I have the same fears as people who do take these precautions, and my window-panes are thin as rime, could shatter like a wineglass. A woman was murdered (how do they put it) in broad daylight in a house two blocks away, last year, and the fierce dogs who guarded an old widower and his collection of antique clocks were strangled before he was knifed by a casual labourer he had dismissed without pay.

I was staring at the door, making it out in my mind rather than seeing it, in the dark. I lay quite still – a victim already – but the arrhythmia of my heart was fleeing, knocking this way and that against its body-cage. How finely tuned the senses are, just out of rest, sleep! I could never listen intently as that in the distractions of the day;

I was reading every faintest sound, identifying and classifying its possible threat.

But I learned that I was to be neither threatened nor spared. There was no human weight pressing on the boards, the creaking was a buckling, an epicentre of stress. I was in it. The house that surrounds me while I sleep is built on undermined ground; far beneath my bed, the floor, the house's foundations, the stopes and passages of gold mines have hollowed the rock, and when some face trembles, detaches and falls, three thousand feet below, the whole house shifts slightly, bringing uneasy strain to the balance and counterbalance of brick, cement, wood and glass that hold it as a structure around me. The misbeats of my heart tailed off like the last muffled flourishes on one of the wooden xylophones made by the Chopi and Tsonga migrant miners who might have been down there, under me in the earth at that moment. The stope where the fall was could have been disused, dripping water from its ruptured veins; or men might now be interred there in the most profound of tombs.

I couldn't find a position in which my mind would let go of my body – release me to sleep again. So I began to tell myself a story; a bedtime story.

In a house, in a suburb, in a city, there were a man and his wife who loved each other very much and were living happily ever after. They had a little boy, and they loved him very much. They had a cat and a dog that the little boy loved very much. They had a car and a caravan trailer for holidays, and a swimming-pool which was fenced so that the little boy and his playmates would not fall in and drown. They had a housemaid who was absolutely trustworthy and an itinerant gardener who was highly recommended by the neighbours. For when they began to live happily ever after they were warned, by that wise old witch, the husband's mother, not to take on anyone off the street. They were inscribed in a medical benefit society, their pet dog was licensed, they were insured against fire, flood damage and theft, and subscribed to the local Neighbourhood Watch, which supplied them with a plaque for their gates lettered YOU HAVE BEEN WARNED over the silhouette of a would-be intruder. He was masked; it could not be said if he was black or white, and therefore proved the property owner was no racist.

It was not possible to insure the house, the swimming pool or the car against riot damage. There were riots, but these were outside the city, where people of another colour were quartered. These people were not allowed into the suburb except as reliable housemaids and gardeners, so there was nothing to fear, the husband told the wife. Yet she was afraid that some day such people might come up the street and tear off the plaque YOU HAVE BEEN WARNED and open the gates and stream in ... Nonsense, my dear, said the husband, there are police and soldiers and tear-gas and guns to keep them away. But to please her – for he loved her very much and buses were being burned, cars stoned, and schoolchildren shot by the police in those quarters out of sight and hearing of the suburb – he had electronically-controlled gates fitted. Anyone who pulled off the sign YOU HAVE BEEN WARNED and tried to open the gates would have to announce his intentions by pressing a button and speaking into a receiver relayed to the house. The little boy was fascinated by the device and used it as a walkie-talkie in cops and robbers play with his small friends.

The riots were suppressed, but there were many burglaries in the suburb and somebody's trusted housemaid was tied up and shut in a cupboard by thieves while she was in charge of her employers' house. The trusted housemaid of the man and wife and little boy was so upset by this misfortune befalling a friend left, as she herself often was, with responsibility for the possessions of the man and his wife and the little boy that she implored her employers to have burglar bars attached to the doors and windows of the house, and an alarm system installed. The wife said, She is right, let us take heed of her advice. So from every window and door in the house where they were living happily ever after they now saw the trees and sky through bars, and when the little boy's pet cat tried to climb in by the fanlight to keep him company in his little bed at night, as it customarily had done, it set off the alarm keening through the house.

The alarm was often answered – it seemed – by other burglar alarms, in other houses, that had been triggered by pet cats or nibbling mice. The alarms called to one another across the gardens in shrills and bleats and wails that everyone soon became accustomed to, so that the din roused the inhabitants of the suburb no more than the croak of frogs and musical grating of cicadas' legs. Under cover of the electronic harpies' discourse intruders sawed the iron bars and broke into homes, taking away hi-fi equipment, television sets, cassette players, cameras and radios, jewellery and clothing, and sometimes were hungry enough to devour everything in the refrigerator or paused audaciously to drink the whisky in the cabinets or patio bars. Insurance companies paid no compensation for single malt, a loss made keener by the property owner's knowledge that the thieves wouldn't even have been able to appreciate what it was they were drinking.

Then the time came when many of the people who were not trusted housemaids and gardeners hung about the suburb because they were unemployed. Some importuned for a job: weeding or painting a roof; anything, *baas*, madam. But the man and his wife remembered the warning about taking on anyone off the street. Some drank liquor and fouled the streets with discarded bottles. Some begged, waiting for the man or his wife to drive the car out of the electronically-operated gates. They sat about with their feet in the gutters, under the jacaranda trees that made a green tunnel of the street – for it was a beautiful suburb, spoilt only by their presence – and sometimes they fell asleep lying right before the gates in the midday sun. The wife could never see anyone go hungry. She sent the trusted housemaid out with bread and tea, but the trusted housemaid said these were loafers and *tsotsis*, who would come and tie her up and shut her in a cupboard. The husband said, She's right. Take heed of her advice. You only encourage them with your bread and tea. They are looking for their chance ... And he brought the little boy's tricycle from the garden into the house every night, because if the house was surely secure, once locked and with the alarm set, someone might still be able to climb over the wall or the electronically-closed gates into the garden.

You are right, said the wife, then the wall should be higher. And the wise old witch, the husband's mother, paid for the extra bricks as her Christmas present to her son and his wife – the little boy got a Space Man outfit and a book of fairy tales.

But every week there were more reports of intrusion: in broad daylight and the dead of night, in the early hours of the morning, and even in the lovely summer twilight – a certain family was at dinner while the bedrooms were being ransacked upstairs. The man and his wife, talking of the latest armed robbery in the suburb, were distracted by the sight of the little boy's pet cat effortlessly arriving over the seven-foot wall, descending first with a rapid bracing of extended forepaws down on the sheer vertical surface, and then a graceful launch, landing with swishing tail within the property. The whitewashed wall was marked with the cat's comings and goings; and on the street side of the wall there were larger red-earth smudges that could have been made by the kind of broken running shoes, seen on the feet of unemployed loiterers, that had no innocent destination.

When the man and wife and little boy took the pet dog for its walk round the neighbourhood streets they no longer paused to admire this show of roses or that perfect lawn; these were hidden behind an array of different varieties of security fences, walls and devices. The man, wife, little boy and dog passed a remarkable choice: there was the low-cost option of pieces of broken glass embedded in cement along the top of walls, there were iron grilles ending in lance-points, there were attempts at reconciling the aesthetics of prison architecture with the Spanish Villa style (spikes painted pink) and with the plaster urns of neo-classical façades (twelve-inch pikes finned like zigzags of lightning and painted pure white). Some walls had a small board affixed, giving the name and telephone number of the firm responsible for the installation of the devices. While the little boy and the pet dog raced ahead, the husband and wife found themselves comparing the poss-ible effectiveness of each style against its appearance; and after several weeks when they paused before this barricade or that without needing to speak, both came out with the conclusion that only one was worth considering. It was the ugliest but the most honest in its suggestion of the pure concentration-camp style, no frills, all evident efficacy. Placed the length of walls, it consisted of a continuous coil of stiff and shining metal serrated into jagged blades, so that there would be no way of climbing over it and no way through its tunnel without getting entangled in its fangs. There would be no way out, only a struggle getting bloodier and bloodier, a deeper and sharper hooking and tearing of flesh. The wife shuddered to look at it. You're right, said the husband, anyone would think twice ... And they took heed of the advice on a small board fixed to the wall: Consult DRAGON'S TEETH The People For Total Security.

Next day a gang of workmen came and stretched the razor-bladed coils all round the walls of the house where the husband and wife and little boy and pet dog and cat were living happily ever after. The sunlight flashed and slashed, off the serrations, the cornice of razor thorns encircled the home, shining. The husband said, Never mind. It will weather. The wife said, You're wrong. They guarantee it's rust-proof. And she waited until the little boy had run off to play before she said, I hope the cat will take heed ... The husband said, Don't worry, my dear, cats always look before they leap. And it was true that from that day on the cat slept in the little boy's bed and kept to the garden, never risking a try at breaching security.

One evening, the mother read the little boy to sleep with a fairy story from the book the wise old witch had given him at Christmas. Next day he pretended to be the Prince who braves the terrible thicket of thorns to enter the palace and kiss the Sleeping Beauty back to life: he dragged a ladder to the wall, the shining coiled tunnel was just wide enough for his little body to creep in, and with the first fixing of its razor-teeth in his knees and hands and head he screamed and struggled deeper into its tangle. The trusted housemaid and the itinerant gardener, whose 'day' it was, came running, the first to see and to scream with him, and the itinerant gardener tore his hands trying to get at the little boy. Then the man and his wife burst wildly into the garden and for some reason (the cat, probably) the alarm set up wailing against the screams while the bleeding mass of the little boy was hacked out of the security coil with saws, wire-cutters, choppers, and they carried it – the man, the wife, the hysterical trusted housemaid and the weeping gardener – into the house.

Shirley Jackson

Shirley Jackson was born in 1919 in San Francisco, California. She began writing as a child, keeping a record of her experiences throughout most of her teenage years. She won a place at Syracuse University, New York, graduating in 1940.

She married in the same year, to Stanley Hyman, with whom she had founded a literary magazine just a few months before. They had four children together. Shirley Jackson never stopped writing, producing six novels, prose and drama for children, as well as numerous short stories and screen plays.

Her stories frequently centre on women characters, not quite at ease with the communities they find themselves in, and where the surface features of everyday life do not match the harsher realities lying just below the surface.

In the 1950s she wrote, with her husband, two semi-autobiographical accounts of family lie, *Life Among the Savages* and *Raising Demons*. Perhaps the story selected here, 'Charles', owes something to this period of her life? She died in 1965.

Charles

Shirley Jackson

The day my son Laurie started kindergarten he renounced corduroy overalls with bibs and began wearing blue jeans with a belt; I watched him go off the first morning with the older girl next door, seeing clearly that an era of my life was ended, my sweet-voiced nursery-school tot replaced by a long-trousered, swaggering character who forgot to stop at the corner and wave good-bye to me.

He came home the same way, the front door slamming open, his cap on the floor, and the voice suddenly become raucous shouting, 'Isn't anybody *here*?'

At lunch he spoke insolently to his father, spilled his baby sister's milk, and remarked that his teacher said we were not to take the name of the Lord in vain.

'How *was* school today?' I asked, elaborately casual.

'All right,' he said.

'Did you learn anything?' his father asked.

Laurie regarded his father coldly. 'I didn't learn nothing,' he said.

'Anything,' I said. 'Didn't learn anything.'

'The teacher spanked a boy, though,' Laurie said, addressing his bread and butter. 'For being fresh,' he added, with his mouth full.

'What did he do?' I asked. 'Who was it?'

Laurie thought. 'It was Charles,' he said. 'He was fresh. The teacher spanked him and made him stand in a corner. He was awfully fresh.'

'What did he do?' I asked again, but Laurie slid off his chair, took a cookie, and left, while his father was still saying, 'See here, young man.'

The next day Laurie remarked at lunch, as soon as he

sat down, 'Well, Charles was bad again today.' He grinned enormously and said, 'Today Charles hit the teacher.'

'Good heavens,' I said, mindful of the Lord's name, 'I suppose he got spanked again?'

'He sure did,' Laurie said. 'Look up,' he said to his father.

'What?' his father said, looking up.

'Look down,' Laurie said. 'Look at my thumb. Gee, you're dumb.' He began to laugh insanely.

'Why did Charles hit the teacher?' I asked quickly.

'Because she tried to make him color with red crayons,' Laurie said. 'Charles wanted to color with green crayons so he hit the teacher and she spanked him and said nobody play with Charles but everybody did.'

The third day – it was Wednesday of the first week – Charles bounced a see-saw on to the head of a little girl and made her bleed, and the teacher made him stay inside all during recess. Thursday Charles had to stand in a corner during story-time because he kept pounding his feet on the floor. Friday Charles was deprived of blackboard privileges because he threw chalk.

On Saturday I remarked to my husband, 'Do you think kindergarten is too unsettling for Laurie? All this toughness, and bad grammar, and this Charles boy sounds like such a bad influence.'

'It'll be all right,' my husband said reassuringly. 'Bound to be people like Charles in the world. Might as well meet them now as later.'

On Monday Laurie came home late, full of news. 'Charles,' he shouted as he came up the hill; I was waiting anxiously on the front steps. 'Charles,' Laurie yelled all the way up the hill, 'Charles was bad again.'

'Come right in,' I said, as soon as he came close enough. 'Lunch is waiting.'

'You know what Charles did?' he demanded, following me through the door. 'Charles yelled so in school they sent a boy in from first grade to tell the teacher she had to make Charles keep quiet, and so Charles had to stay after school. And so all the children stayed to watch him.'

'What did he do?' I asked.

'He just sat there,' Laurie said, climbing into his chair at the table. 'Hi, Pop, y'old dust mop.'

'Charles had to stay after school today,' I told my husband. 'Everyone stayed with him.'

'What does this Charles look like?' my husband asked Laurie. 'What's his other name?'

'He's bigger than me,' Laurie said. 'And he doesn't have any rubbers and he doesn't ever wear a jacket.'

Monday night was the first Parent-Teachers meeting, and only the fact that the baby had a cold kept me from going; I wanted passionately to meet Charles's mother. On Tuesday Laurie remarked suddenly, 'Our teacher had a friend come to see her in school today.'

'Charles's mother?' my husband and I asked simultaneously.

'Naaah,' Laurie said scornfully. 'It was a man who came and made us do exercises, we had to touch our toes. Look.' He climbed down from his chair and squatted down and touched his toes. 'Like this,' he said. He got solemnly back into his chair and said, picking up his fork, 'Charles didn't even *do* exercises.'

'That's fine,' I said heartily. 'Didn't Charles want to do exercises?'

'Naaah,' Laurie said. 'Charles was so fresh to the teacher's friend he wasn't *let* do exercises.'

'Fresh again?' I said.

'He kicked the teacher's friend,' Laurie said. 'The teacher's friend told Charles to touch his toes like I just did and Charles kicked him.'

'What are they going to do about Charles, do you suppose?' Laurie's father asked him.

Laurie shrugged elaborately. 'Throw him out of school, I guess,' he said.

Wednesday and Thursday were routine; Charles yelled during story hour and hit a boy in the stomach and made him cry. On Friday Charles stayed after school again and so did all the other children.

With the third week of kindergarten Charles was an institution in our family; the baby was being a Charles when she cried all afternoon; Laurie did a Charles when he filled his wagon full of mud and pulled it through the kitchen; even my husband, when he caught his elbow in the telephone cord and pulled telephone, ashtray, and a bowl of flowers off the table, said, after the first minute, 'Looks like Charles.'

During the third and fourth weeks it looked like a reformation in Charles; Laurie reported grimly at lunch on Thursday of the third week, 'Charles was so good today the teacher gave him an apple.'

'What?' I said, and my husband added warily, 'You mean Charles?'

'Charles,' Laurie said. 'He gave the crayons around and he picked up the books afterward and the teacher said he was her helper.'

'What happened?' I asked incredulously.

'He was her helper, that's all,' Laurie said, and shrugged.

'Can this be true, about Charles?' I asked my husband that night. 'Can something like this happen?'

'Wait and see,' my husband said cynically. 'When you've got a Charles to deal with, this may mean he's only plotting.'

He seemed to be wrong. For over a week Charles was the teacher's helper; each day he handed things out and he picked things up; no one had to stay after school.

'The PTA meeting's next week again,' I told my husband one evening. 'I'm going to find Charles's mother there.'

'Ask her what happened to Charles,' my husband said. 'I'd like to know.'

'I'd like to know myself,' I said.

On Friday of that week things were back to normal. 'You know what Charles did today?' Laurie demanded at the lunch table, in a voice slightly awed. 'He told a little girl to say a word and she said it and the teacher washed her mouth out with soap and Charles laughed.'

'What word?' his father asked unwisely, and Laurie said, 'I'll have to whisper it to you, it's so bad.' He got down off his chair and went around to his father. His father bent his head down and Laurie whispered joyfully. His father's eyes widened.

'Did Charles tell the little girl to say *that*?' he asked respectfully.

'She said it *twice*,' Laurie said. 'Charles told her to say it *twice*.'

'What happened to Charles?' my husband asked.

'Nothing,' Laurie said. 'He was passing out the crayons.'

Monday morning Charles abandoned the little girl and said the evil word himself three or four times, getting his mouth washed out with soap each time. He also threw chalk.

My husband came to the door with me that evening as I set out for the PTA meeting. 'Invite her over for a cup of tea after the meeting,' he said. 'I want to get a look at her.'

'If only she's there,' I said prayerfully.

'She'll be there,' my husband said. 'I don't see how they could hold a PTA meeting without Charles's mother.'

At the meeting I sat restlessly, scanning each comfortable matronly face, trying to determine which one hid the secret of Charles. None of them looked to me haggard enough. No one stood up in the meeting and apologized for the way her son had been acting. No one mentioned Charles.

After the meeting I identified and sought out Laurie's kindergarten teacher. She had a plate with a cup of tea and a piece of chocolate cake; I had a plate with a cup of tea and a piece of marshmallow cake. We maneuvered up to one another cautiously, and smiled.

'I've been so anxious to meet you,' I said. 'I'm Laurie's mother.'

'We're all so interested in Laurie,' she said.

'Well, he certainly likes kindergarten,' I said. 'He talks about it all the time.'

'We had a little trouble adjusting, the first week or so,' she said primly, 'but now he's a fine little helper. With occasional lapses, of course.'

'Laurie usually adjusts very quickly,' I said. 'I suppose this time it's Charles's influence.'

'Charles?'

'Yes,' I said, laughing, 'you must have your hands full in that kindergarten, with Charles.'

'Charles?' she said. 'We don't have any Charles in the kindergarten.'

Penelope Lively

Penelope Lively was born in Egypt in 1933 but settled in England after the Second World War. She was at Oxford University in the 1950s, and took a degree in modern history in 1956. She married a university teacher in 1957 and has lived around the Oxfordshire area ever since. She has one daughter and a son.

Penelope Lively's first novel *Astercote* was published in 1970, but she quickly established herself as being one of the most interesting of contemporary novelists for children. *The Ghost of Thomas Kempe* (1973) is perhaps the best known as it won the prestigious Carnegie Award, but *The House in Norham Gardens* (1974) and *Going Back* (1975) are equally rewarding.

Penelope Lively's writing often evokes a strong sense of place, usually generated through the processes of remembering. She has commented that 'All my books for children reflect in one way or another, my own interest in the workings of memory – whether personal or collective. They all come out differently, but somehow the theme has persisted.'

Since 1977, Penelope Lively has concentrated on writing adult fiction, where her Oxbridge links have allowed her to observe the upper-middle classes with a shrewd sense of detachment and understanding.

The story selected here, 'Next Term We'll Mash You' is from her first collection of short stories *Nothing Missing But The Samovar* (1978).

Next term, we'll mash you

Penelope Lively

Inside the car it was quiet, the noise of the engine even
and subdued, the air just the right temperature, the
windows tight-fitting. The boy sat on the back seat, a box
of chocolates, unopened, beside him, and a comic, folded.
The trim Sussex landscape flowed past the windows: cows,
white-fenced fields, highly-priced period houses. The sunlight was glassy, remote as a coloured photograph. The
backs of the two heads in front of him swayed with the
motion of the car.

His mother half-turned to speak to him. 'Nearly there
now, darling.'

The father glanced downwards at his wife's wrist. 'Are
we all right for time?'

'Just right. Nearly twelve.'

'I could do with a drink. Hope they lay something on.'

'I'm sure they will. The Wilcoxes say they're awfully nice
people. Not really the schoolmaster-type at all, Sally says.

The man said, 'He's an Oxford chap.'

'Is he? You didn't say.'

'Mmn.'

'Of course, the fees are that much higher than the
Seaford place.'

'Fifty quid or so. We'll have to see.'

The car turned right, between white gates and high,
dark, tight-clipped hedges. The whisper of the road under
the tyres changed to the crunch of gravel. The child,
staring sideways, read black lettering on a white board: 'St
Edward's Preparatory School. Please Drive Slowly'. He
shifted on the seat, and the leather sucked at the bare skin
under his knees, stinging.

The mother said, 'It's a lovely place. Those must be the

playing-fields. Look, darling, there are some of the boys.'
She clicked open her handbag, and the sun caught her
mirror and flashed in the child's eyes; the comb went
through her hair and he saw the grooves it left, neat as
distant ploughing.

'Come on, then, Charles, out you get.'

The building was red brick, early nineteenth century,
spreading out long arms in which windows glittered
blackly. Flowers, trapped in neat beds, were alternate red
and white. They went up the steps, the man, the woman,
and the child two paces behind.

The woman, the mother, smoothing down a skirt that
would be ridged from sitting, thought: I like the way
they've got the maid all done up properly. The little white
apron and all that. She's foreign, I suppose. Au pair. Very
nice. If he comes here there'll be Speech Days and that
kind of thing. Sally Wilcox says it's quite dressy – she got
that cream linen coat for coming down here. You can see
why it costs a bomb. Great big grounds and only an hour
and a half from London.

They went into a room looking out into a terrace.
Beyond, dappled lawns, gently shifting trees, black and
white cows grazing behind iron railings. Books, leather
chairs, a table with magazines – *Country Life*, *The Field*,
The Economist. 'Please, if you would wait here. The Headmaster won't be long.'

Alone, they sat, inspected. 'I like the atmosphere, don't
you, John?'

'Very pleasant, yes.' Four hundred a term, near enough.
You can tell it's a cut above the Seaford place, though, or
the one at St Albans. Bob Wilcox says quite a few City
people send their boys here. One or two of the merchant
bankers, those kind of people. It's the sort of contact that
would do no harm at all. You meet someone, get talking at
a cricket match or what have you ... Not at all a bad
thing.

'All right, Charles? You didn't get sick in the car, did
you?'

The child had black hair, slicked down smooth to his
head. His ears, too large, jutted out, transparent in the
light from the window, laced with tiny, delicate veins. His

clothes had the shine and crease of newness. He looked at the books, the dark brown pictures, his parents, said nothing.

'Come here, let me tidy your hair.'

The door opened. The child hesitated, stood up, sat, then rose again with his father.

'Mr and Mrs Manders? How very nice to meet you – I'm Margaret Spokes, and will you please forgive my husband who is tied up with some wretch who broke the cricket pavilion window and will be just a few more minutes. We try to be organised but a schoolmaster's day is always just that bit unpredictable. Do please sit down and what will you have to revive you after that beastly drive? You live in Finchley, is that right?'

'Hampstead, really,' said the mother. 'Sherry would be lovely.' She worked over the headmaster's wife from shoes to hairstyle, pricing and assessing. Shoes old but expensive – Russell and Bromley. Good skirt. Blouse could be Marks and Sparks – not sure. Real pearls. Super Victorian ring. She's not gone to any particular trouble – that's just what she'd wear anyway. You can be confident, with a voice like that, of course. Sally Wilcox says she knows all sorts of people.

The headmaster's wife said, 'I don't know how much you know about us? Prospectuses don't tell you a thing do they. We'll look round everything in a minute, when you've had a chat with my husband. I gather you're friends of the Wilcoxes, by the way. I'm awfully fond of Simon – he's down for Winchester, of course, but I expect you know that.'

The mother smiled over her sherry. Oh, I know that all right. Sally Wilcox doesn't let you forget that.

'And this is Charles? My dear, we've been forgetting all about you! In a minute I'm going to borrow Charles and take him off to meet some of the boys because after all you're choosing a school for him, aren't you, and not for you, so he ought to know what he might be letting himself in for and it shows we've got nothing to hide.'

The parents laughed. The father, sherry warming his guts, thought that this was an amusing woman. Not attractive, of course, a bit homespun, but impressive all the same. Partly the voice, of course; it takes a bloody expensive education to produce a voice like that. And other things, of course. Background and all that stuff.

'I think I can hear the thud of the Fourth Form coming in from games, which means my husband is on his way, and then I shall leave you with him while I take Charles off to the common room.'

For a moment the three adults centred on the child, looking, judging. The mother said, 'He looks so hideously pale, compared to those boys we saw outside.'

'My dear, that's London, isn't it? You just have to get them out, to get some colour into them. Ah, here's James. James – Mr and Mrs Manders. You remember, Bob Wilcox was mentioning at Sports Day . . .

The headmaster reflected his wife's style, like paired cards in Happy Families. His clothes were mature rather than old, his skin well-scrubbed, his shoes clean, his geniality untainted by the least condescension. He was genuinely sorry to have kept them waiting, but in this business one lurches from one minor crisis to the next . . . And this is Charles? Hello, there, Charles. His large hand rested for a moment on the child's head, quite extinguishing the thin, dark hair. It was as though he had but to clench his fingers to crush the skull. But he took his hand away and moved the parents to the window, to observe the mutilated cricket pavilion, with indulgent laughter.

And the child is borne away by the headmaster's wife. She never touches him or tells him to come, but simply bears him away like some relentless tide, down corridors and through swinging glass doors, towing him like a frail craft, not bothering to look back to see if he is following, confident in the strength of magnetism, or obedience.

And delivers him to a room where boys are scattered among inky tables and rungless chairs and sprawled on a mangy carpet. There is a scampering, and a rising, and a silence falling, as she opens the door.

'Now this is the Lower Third, Charles, who you'd be with if you come to us in September. Boys, this is Charles Manders, and I want you to tell him all about things and answer any questions he wants to ask. You can believe about half of what they say, Charles, and they will tell you the most fearful lies about the food, which is excellent.'

The boys laugh and groan; amiable, exaggerated groans. They must like the headmaster's wife: there is licensed repartee. They look at her with bright eyes in open, eager faces. Someone leaps to hold the door for her, and close it behind her. She is gone.

The child stands in the centre of the room, and it draws in around him. The circle of children contracts, faces are only a yard or so from him, strange faces, looking, assessing.

Asking questions. They help themselves to his name, his age, his school. Over their heads he sees beyond the window an inaccessible world of shivering trees and high racing clouds and his voice which has floated like a feather in the dusty schoolroom air dies altogether and he becomes mute, and he stands in the middle of them with shoulders humped, staring down at feet: grubby plimsolls and kicked brown sandals. There is a noise in his ears like rushing water, a torrential din out of which voices boom, blotting each other out so that he cannot always hear the words. Do you? they say, and Have you? and What's your? and the faces, if he looks up, swing into one another in kaleidoscopic patterns and the floor under his feet is unsteady, lifting and falling.

And out of the noises comes one voice that is complete, that he can hear. 'Next term we'll mash you,' it says. 'We always mash new boys.'

And a bell goes, somewhere beyond doors and down corridors, and suddenly the children are all gone, clattering away and leaving him there with the heaving floor and the walls that shift and swing, and the headmaster's wife comes back and tows him away, and he is with his parents again, and they are getting into the car, and the high hedges skim past the car windows once more, in the other direction, and the gravel under the tyres changes to black tarmac.

'Well?'

'I liked it, didn't you?' The mother adjusted the car around her, closing windows, shrugging into her seat.

'Very pleasant, really. Nice chap.'

'I like him. Not quite so sure about her.'

'It's pricey, of course.'

'All the same . . .'

'Money well spent, though. One way and another.'

'Shall we settle it, then?'

'I think so. I'll drop him a line.'

The mother pitched her voice a notch higher to speak to the child in the back of the car. 'Would you like to go there, Charles? Like Simon Wilcox. Did you see that lovely gym, and the swimming-pool? And did the other boys tell you all about it?'

The child does not answer. He looks straight ahead of him, at the road coiling beneath the bonnet of the car. His face is haggard with anticipation.

Janet Frame

Janet Frame was born in Dunedin in New Zealand in 1924. She is the third of five children; two of her sisters were tragically drowned in separate accidents during their adolescence. Janet was the first child of the family to reach high school, and in 1943 she went on to Dunedin Teachers College. She did not take to teaching, and in her first year walked out of the classroom, never to return.

In Frame's family, 'writing was an accepted pastime'; her mother, particularly, wrote poems, songs and stories. Frame's first published stories appeared in 1951. She has established a considerable body of work since that time, including twelve novels, three collections of short stories and sketches, a volume of poetry and a book for children.

Janet Frame's mental health has been fragile over the years, and she has spent a good deal of time in hospital. In 1947 she voluntarily entered Seacliff Psychiatric Hospital and remained in psychiatric hospitals for the next eight years. In 1957 she left New Zealand and travelled to Ibiza and then to London on a State Literary Fund grant. In London doctors confirmed that she was not in fact schizophrenic. In 1961 *Faces in the Water* was published, a novel in which she explored some of her experiences in hospital.

Janet Frame's personal story of loneliness, despair and later success and recognition as a writer is charted in her three part autobiography: *To the Is-land*, published in 1983; *An Angel at my Table* published in 1984 and the third volume, *The Envoy from the Mirror City* published in 1985. This autobiographical work has formed the basis for a highly acclaimed film and television programme.

Her short story 'Stink-pot' gives us a glimpse into the troubled emotions of childhood.

Stink-pot

Janet Frame

Someone began to call my sister stink-pot. Soon all the children at school were calling her Stink-pot with the result that, gumming events together and tying possibilities like the tails of paper kites, they began to call out to me, all along Reed Street and Ribble Street and down Dee Street where Beverly Willis lived who had been to Australia. 'You're Stink-pot Wellaby's sister.'

To tell the truth our name was not Wellaby but one of my secret longings was to have a name with three syllables, therefore I have named us Wellaby.

'You're Stink-pot Wellaby's sister!'

See how distinguished it looks and sounds. But all the same it was an insult.

At first I was indignant and defended the rights of my family by retaliating with a feeble 'She's not a Stink-pot.' Then, growing cunning, for affairs were not as peaceful as they should have been between Molly and me, I introduced her new label into our home, to protect myself against bullying or sly elder-sister manoeuvres.

'Stink-pot,' I said.

'Mum, Nini's called me Stink-pot!'

From the kitchen came my mother's voice answering, 'Don't quarrel, kiddies. Love one another. Say nice words to each other!'

How I hated my mother! There was never any variation in her advice, it was always, Love one another, and at night when darkness threatened it was always, Think about nice things, about sunshine and fairies.

Sunshine and fairies! I never knew fairies, and if I did I would not have cared to invite them to my dreams unless they proved themselves capable of engaging in more

interesting activities than sitting around on flower petals
in ballet dresses, waving wands in the air.

'Stink-pot,' I said again to Molly, this time in response
to a particularly annoying and painful arm-twist which
nearly crippled me.

'Mum, she's called me Stink-pot again!'

This time there was no answer from my mother. She
had gone outside to the garden or the clothesline.

Then my sister found a new defense against me.

'All right,' she said, with an air of clinching things. She
began to chant,

> Sticks and stones will break my bones,
> but names will never hurt me,
> and when I'm dead and in my grave,
> you'll hear the names you called me!

There was something in that rhyme which frightened
me, yet I questioned its truthfulness.

'How can I hear the names when you're dead and gone?'

'They'll go over and over in your head. They'll knock at
your door lift up the latch walk in; all the names you've
ever called me in your life from when you were the size of
a flea.'

'I never was the size of a flea.'

'That's all *you* know about it. You were the size of a
peanut, a monkeynut, same thing ha ha, and a grape and
a spider and a flea and an earwig with a copper overcoat.'

'I never was. I don't often call you names, anyway.'

'You do. What about S-T-I-N-K [she was spelling it out]
P-O-T?'

I grew daring. 'Stink-pot, Stink-pot!' I cried.

'You'll see,' Molly said. 'You'll see when I'm dead and
gone and in my grave.'

And she twisted my arm once more, and caught at my
wrist, giving me a vicious Chinese and Maori burn
combined.

There was no precedent. Molly died. And not long after her
death I was lying in bed one night waiting for the names
to come after me. If they're going to haunt me, and I'm

going to hear them, it will be now, I thought. It will be tonight. I waited.

> Sticks and stones will break my bones,
> but names will never hurt me,
> and when I'm dead and in my grave
> you'll hear the names you called me.

I listened hard, considering the possibilities. Molly was dead and in her grave; the requirements of the verse were complete. I had said 'No' when my mother asked, 'Do you want to look at Molly before she is buried?' I was wishing now that I hadn't said 'No.' But she had been lying in the room amongst the smell of sturmer apples, and that had seemed strange. I supposed that at that very moment she was sending out the lists of names as quickly as she could, wasting no time, now that she was dead and in her grave. Besides Stink-pot I remembered Knock-knees, Pick-the-Pie, loony, greedy-guts, Fatty Arbuckle, Bandy-legs, not to mention the names of all the boys she had been sweet on, starting from Harry Hunt and ending up with Ted Hamilton.

I was lonely in the big bed that night. I unscrewed one of the knobs at the foot of the bed and picked out the piece of paper with the code message that we had posted to each other weeks ago. Alas, it was so long ago that we had played that game, I couldn't understand the message, I had forgotten the code.

I tore up the message.

Then I lay down again, waiting for the names. When I'm dead and in my grave you'll hear the names you called me. I knew that if I were going to hear them at all it would be that night, for Molly had been dead long enough to have arranged everything, every kind of revenge and torture. I knew for certain that if the names came it would be then, as I lay alone in the big bed, listening to the owls in the trees, and the small birds calling suddenly, startled from their sleep in the hedge.

I listened so hard, holding my breath in case I blew away the sound. I had gathered from Molly's chanting that when I did hear the names the experience would be very unpleasant, and perhaps would even drive me, in my turn, to the grave.

I wondered if Molly were feeling cold, if she were hungry or thirsty, if she remembered the code message hidden in the bed-knob and could translate the code.

And all the time I was listening for the names. I listened so hard, all night until the early morning. And I heard no names, not one name, not even Stink-pot.

In the end I turned over to go to sleep. I always knew Molly was a liar.

'Liar, liar!' I whispered triumphantly into my pillow.

Anita Desai

Anita Desai was born in India in 1937, the daughter of a Bengali father and a German mother. She went first to school, then to University in Delhi but now lives in Bombay, which is the setting for most of her short stories including 'Games at Twilight.'

Married with four children, Anita Desai started to write at an early age. 'I have been writing, since the age of seven, as instinctively as I breathe. It is a necessity to me. I find it is in the process of writing that I am able to think, to feel, and to realise at the highest pitch.'

Like many other contemporary Indian writers, Anita Desai writes in English. She has written many novels and short stories for adult readers, a good example being *Fire On The Mountain* (1977). She has also written a variety of award winning works for children, the best known perhaps being *The Village by the Sea* (1982).

Children and the peculiarly intense world of childhood, feature prominently in many of her short stories, including the example offered here, 'Games at Twilight.' The setting for this story is a garden in a prosperous Bombay suburb but the actions which follow could happen anywhere.

Games at Twilight

Anita Desai

It was still too hot to play outdoors. They had had their tea, they had been washed and had their hair brushed, and after the long day of confinement in the house that was not cool but at least a protection from the sun, the children strained to get out. Their faces were red and bloated with the effort, but their mother would not open the door, everything was still curtained and shuttered in a way that stifled the children, made them feel that their lungs were stuffed with cotton wool and their noses with dust and if they didn't burst out into the light and see the sun and feel the air, they would choke.

'Please, ma, please,' they begged. 'We'll play in the veranda and porch – we won't go a step out of the porch.'

'You will, I know you will, and then – '

'No – we won't, we won't,' they wailed so horrendously that she actually let down the bolt of the front door so that they burst out like seeds from a crackling, over-ripe pod into the veranda, with such wild, maniacal yells that she retreated to her bath and the shower of talcum powder and the fresh sari that were to help her face the summer evening.

They faced the afternoon. It was too hot. Too bright. The white walls of the veranda glared stridently in the sun. The bougainvillea hung about it, purple and magenta, in livid balloons. The garden outside was like a tray made of beaten brass, flattened out on the red gravel and the stony soil in all shades of metal – aluminium, tin, copper and brass. No life stirred at this arid time of day – the birds still drooped, like dead fruit, in the papery tents of the trees; some squirrels lay limp on the wet earth under the

garden tap. The outdoor dog lay stretched as if dead on the
veranda mat, his paws and ears and tail all reaching out
like dying travellers in search of water. He rolled his eyes
at the children – two white marbles rolling in the purple
sockets, begging for sympathy – and attempted to lift his
tail in a wag but could not. It only twitched and lay still.

Then, perhaps roused by the shrieks of the children, a
band of parrots suddenly fell out of the eucalyptus tree,
tumbled frantically in the still, sizzling air, then sorted
themselves out into battle formation and streaked away
across the white sky.

The children, too, felt released. They too began tumbling,
shoving, pushing against each other, frantic to start. Start
what? Start their business. The business of the children's
day which is – play.

'Let's play hide-and-seek.'

'Who'll be It?'

'You be It.'

'Why should I? You be – '

'You're the eldest – '

'That doesn't mean – '

The shoves became harder. Some kicked out. The moth-
erly Mira intervened. She pulled the boys roughly apart.
There was a tearing sound of cloth but it was lost in the
heavy panting and angry grumbling and no one paid
attention to the small sleeve hanging loosely off a shoulder.

'Make a circle, make a circle!' she shouted, firmly pulling
and pushing till a kind of vague circle was formed. 'Now
clap!' she roared and, clapping, they all chanted in melancholy unison: 'Dip, dip, dip – my blue ship – ' and every
now and then one or the other saw he was safe by the way
his hands fell at the crucial moment – palm on palm, or
back of hand on palm – and dropped out of the circle with
a yell and a jump of relief and jubilation.

Raghu was It. He started to protest, to cry 'You cheated
– Mira cheated – Anu cheated – ' but it was too late, the
others had all already streaked away. There was no one to
hear when he called out, 'Only in the veranda – the porch
– Ma said – Ma *said* to stay in the porch!' No one had
stopped to listen, all he saw were their brown legs flashing
through the dusty shrubs, scrambling up brick walls,

leaping over compost heaps and hedges, and then the porch stood empty in the purple shade of the bougainvillea and the garden was as empty as before; even the limp squirrels had whisked away, leaving everything gleaming, brassy and bare.

Only small Manu suddenly reappeared, as if he had dropped out of an invisible cloud or from a bird's claws, and stood for a moment in the centre of the yellow lawn, chewing his finger and near to tears as he heard Raghu shouting, with his head pressed against the veranda wall, 'Eighty-three, eighty-five, eighty-nine, ninety . . .' and then made off in a panic, half of him wanting to fly north, the other half counselling south. Raghu turned just in time to see the flash of his white shorts and the uncertain skittering of his red sandals, and charged after him with such a blood-curdling yell that Manu stumbled over the hosepipe, fell into its rubber coils and lay there weeping, 'I won't be It – you have to find them all – all – All!'

'I know I have to, idiot,' Raghu said, superciliously kicking him with his toe. 'You're dead,' he said with satisfaction, licking the beads of perspiration off his upper lip, and then stalked off in search of worthier prey, whistling spiritedly so that the hiders should hear and tremble.

Ravi heard the whistling and picked his nose in a panic, trying to find comfort by burrowing the finger deep-deep into that soft tunnel. He felt himself too exposed, sitting on an upturned flower pot behind the garage. Where could he burrow? He could run around the garage if he heard Raghu come – around and around and around – but he hadn't much faith in his short legs when matched against Raghu's long, hefty, hairy footballer legs. Ravi had a frightening glimpse of them as Raghu combed the hedge of crotons and hibiscus, trampling delicate ferns underfoot as he did so. Ravi looked about him desperately, swallowing a small ball of snot in his fear.

The garage was locked with a great heavy lock to which the driver had the key in his room, hanging from a nail on the wall under his work-shirt. Ravi had peeped in and seen him still sprawling on his string-cot in his vest and striped underpants, the hair on his chest and the hair in his nose shaking with the vibrations of his phlegm-obstructed snores. Ravi had wished he were tall enough, big enough to reach the key on the nail, but it was impossible, beyond his reach for years to come. He had sidled away and sat dejectedly on the flower pot. That at least was cut to his own size.

But next to the garage was another shed with a big green door. Also locked. No one even knew who had the key to the lock. That shed wasn't opened more than once a year when Ma turned out all the old broken bits of furniture and rolls of matting and leaking buckets, and the white ant hills were broken and swept away and Flit sprayed into the spider webs and rat holes so that the whole operation was like the looting of a poor, ruined and conquered city. The green leaves of the door sagged. They were nearly off their rusty hinges. The hinges were large and made a small gap between the door and the walls – only large enough for rats, dogs and, possibly, Ravi to slip through.

Ravi had never cared to enter such a dark and depressing mortuary of defunct household goods seething with such unspeakable and alarming animal life but, as Raghu's whistling grew angrier and sharper and his crashing and storming in the hedge wilder, Ravi suddenly slipped off the flower pot and through the crack and was gone. He chuckled aloud with astonishment at his own temerity so that Raghu came out of the hedge, stood silent with his hands on his hips, listening, and finally shouted 'I heard you! I'm coming! *Got* you – ' and came charging round the garage only to find the upturned flower pot, the yellow dust, the crawling of white ants in a mud-hill against the closed shed door – nothing. Snarling, he bent to pick up a stick and went off, whacking it against the garage and shed walls as if to beat out his prey.

Ravi shook, then shivered with delight, with self-congratulation. Also with fear. It was dark, spooky in the shed. It had a muffled smell, as of graves. Ravi had once got locked into the linen cupboard and sat there weeping for half an hour before he was rescued. But at least that had been a familiar place, and even smelt pleasantly of starch, laundry and, reassuringly, of his mother. But the shed smelt of rats, ant hills, dust and spider webs. Also of less definable, less recognizable horrors. And it was dark. Except for the white-hot cracks along the door, there was no light. The roof was very low. Although Ravi was small, he felt as if he could reach up and touch it with his finger tips. But he didn't stretch. He hunched himself into a ball so as not to bump into anything, touch or feel anything. What might there not be to touch him and feel him as he stood there, trying to see in the dark? Something cold, or slimy – like a snake. Snakes! He leapt up as Raghu whacked the wall with his stick – then, quickly realizing what it was, felt almost relieved to hear Raghu, hear his stick. It made him feel protected.

But Raghu soon moved away. There wasn't a sound once his footsteps had gone around the garage and disappeared. Ravi stood frozen inside the shed. Then he shivered all over. Something had tickled the back of his neck. It took him a while to pick up the courage to lift his hand and explore. It was an insect – perhaps a spider – exploring *him*. He squashed it and wondered how many more creatures were watching him, waiting to reach out and touch him, the stranger.

There was nothing now. After standing in that position – his hand still on his neck, feeling the wet splodge of the squashed spider gradually dry – for minutes, hours, his legs began to tremble with the effort, the inaction. By now he could see enough in the dark to make out the large solid shapes of old wardrobes, broken buckets and bedsteads piled on top of each other around him. He recognized an old bathtub – patches of enamel glimmered at him and at last he lowered himself onto its edge.

He contemplated slipping out of the shed and into the fray. He wondered if it would not be better to be captured by Raghu and be returned to the milling crowd as long as he could be in the sun, the light, the free spaces of the garden and the familiarity of his brothers, sisters and cousins. It would be evening soon. Their games would become legitimate. The parents would sit out on the lawn on cane basket chairs and watch them as they tore around the garden or gathered in knots to share a loot of mulber-

ries or black, teeth-splitting *jamun* from the garden trees.
The gardener would fix the hosepipe to the water tap and
water would fall lavishly through the air to the ground,
soaking the dry yellow grass and the red gravel and
arousing the sweet, the intoxicating scent of water on dry
earth – that loveliest scent in the world. Ravi sniffed for a
whiff of it. He half-rose from the bathrub, then heard the
despairing scream of one of the girls as Raghu bore down
upon her. There was the sound of a crash, and of rolling
about in the bushes, the shrubs, then screams and accus-
ing sobs of, 'I touched the den – ' 'You did not – ' 'I did – '
'You liar, you did *not*' and then a fading away and silence
again.

Ravi sat back on the harsh edge of the tub, deciding to
hold out a bit longer. What fun if they were all found and
caught – he alone left unconquered! He had never known
that sensation. Nothing more wonderful had ever happened to him than being taken out by an uncle and bought
a whole slab of chocolate all to himself, or being flung into
the soda-man's pony cart and driven up to the gate by the
friendly driver with the red beard and pointed ears. To
defeat Raghu – that hirsute, hoarse-voiced football champion – and to be the winner in a circle of older, bigger,
luckier children – that would be thrilling beyond imagin-
ation. He hugged his knees together and smiled to himself
almost shyly at the thought of so much victory, such
laurels.

There he sat smiling, knocking his heels against the
bathtub, now and then getting up and going to the door to
put his ear to the broad crack and listening for sounds of
the game, the pursuer and the pursued, and then returning to his seat with the dogged determination of the true
winner, a breaker of records, a champion.

It grew darker in the shed as the light at the door grew
softer, fuzzier, turned to a kind of crumbling yellow pollen
that turned to yellow fur, blue fur, grey fur. Evening.
Twilight. The sound of water gushing, falling. The scent of
earth receiving water, slaking its thirst in great gulps and
releasing that green scent of freshness, coolness. Through
the crack Ravi saw the long purple shadows of the shed

and the garage lying still across the yard. Beyond that, the white walls of the house. The bougainvillea had lost its lividity, hung in dark bundles that quaked and twittered and seethed with masses of homing sparrows. The lawn was shut off from his view. Could he hear the children's voices? It seemed to him that he could. It seemed to him that he could hear them chanting, singing, laughing. But what about the game? What had happened? Could it be over? How could it when he was still not found?

It then occurred to him that he could have slipped out long ago, dashed across the yard to the veranda and touched the 'den'. It was necessary to do that to win. He had forgotten. He had only remembered the part of hiding and trying to elude the seeker. He had done that so successfully, his success had occupied him so wholly that he had quite forgotten that success had to be clinched by that final dash to victory and the ringing dry of 'Den!'.

With a whimper he burst through the crack, fell on his knees, got up and stumbled on stiff, benumbed legs across the shadowy yard, crying heartily by the time he reached the veranda so that when he flung himself at the white pillar and bawled, 'Den! Den! Den!' his voice broke with rage and pity at the disgrace of it all and he felt himself flooded with tears and misery.

Out on the lawn, the children stopped chanting. They all turned to stare at him in amazement. Their faces were pale and triangular in the dusk. The trees and bushes around them stood inky and sepulchral, spilling long shadows across them. They stared, wondering at his reappearance, his passion, his wild animal howling. Their mother rose from her basket chair and came towards him, worried, annoyed, saying, 'Stop it, stop it, Ravi. Don't be a baby. Have you hurt yourself?' Seeing him attended to, the children went back to clasping their hands and chanting 'The grass is green, the rose is red . . .'

But Ravi would not let them. He tore himself out of his mother's grasp and pounded across the lawn into their midst, charging at them with his head lowered so that they scattered in surprise. 'I won, I won, I won,' he bawled, shaking his head so that the big tears flew. 'Raghu didn't find me. I won, I won —'

It took them a minute to grasp what he was saying, even who he was. They had quite forgotten him. Raghu had found all the others long ago. There had been a fight about who was to be It next. It had been so fierce that their mother had emerged from her bath and made them change to another game. Then they had played another and another. Broken mulberries from the tree and eaten them. Helped the driver wash the car when their father returned from work. Helped the gardener water the beds till he roared at them and swore he would complain to their parents. The parents had come out, taken up their positions on the cane chairs. They had begun to play again, sing and chant. All this time no one had remembered Ravi. Having disappeared from the scene, he had disappeared from their minds. Clean.

'Don't be a fool,' Raghu said roughly, pushing him aside, and even Mira said, 'Stop howling, Ravi. If you want to play, you can stand at the end of the line,' and she put him there very firmly.

The game proceeded. Two pairs of arms reached up and met in an arc. The children trooped under it again and again in a lugubrious circle, ducking their heads and intoning

> 'The grass is green,
> The rose is red;
> Remember me
> When I am dead, dead, dead dead . . .'

And the arc of thin arms trembled in the twilight, and the heads were bowed so sadly, and their feet trampled to that melancholy refrain so mournfully, so helplessly, that Ravi could not bear it. He would not follow them, he would not be included in this funereal game. He had wanted victory and triumph – not a funeral. But he had been forgotten, left out and he would not join them now. The ignominy of being forgotten – how could he face it? He felt his heart go heavy and ache inside him unbearably. He lay down full length on the damp grass, crushing his face into it, no longer crying, silenced by a terrible sense of his insignificance.

Shena Mackay

Shena Mackay was born in Edinburgh in 1945 and grew up in London and Kent. She was already writing when she left school at sixteen and took a series of jobs in a library, factory and antique shop. Shena Mackay is married and has three daughters. She wrote her first books when she was just seventeen: two short novels *Dust Falls On Eugene Schlumberger* and *Toddler on the Run* (1964). The toddler in the story was actually a house-breaking dwarf.

She has published seven novels including *Redhill Rococo* (1986) and her latest *Dunedin* (1992). She has also published three collections of short stories, *Babies in Rhinestones* (1983), *The Laughing Academy* (1993) and *Dreams of Dead Women's Handbags* (1987), from which the story 'Cardboard City' is taken.

Shena Mackay's writing often concentrates on ordinary people in everyday situations, but it is never in the least dull. She finds both menace and humour in examining these ordinary lives in minute detail. 'Cardboard City' follows the story of two sisters who go on a shopping trip to London. Mixed in with the pleasure of a day's outing is the loathing they feel for their new step-father and a desperate longing to see their own father.

Cardboard City

Sheena Mackay

'We could always pick the dog hairs off each other's coats . . .'

The thought of grooming each other like monkeys looking for fleas sent them into giggles – anything would have.

'I used half a roll of Sellotape on mine,' said Stella indignantly then, although she wasn't really offended.

'It better not have been my Sellotape or I'll kill you,' Vanessa responded, without threat.

'It was His.'

'Good. *He'll* kill you then,' she said matter-of-factly.

The sisters, having flung themselves on to the train with no time to buy a comic, were wondering how to pass the long minutes until it reached central London with nothing to read. They could hardly believe that at the last moment He had not contrived to spoil their plan to go Christmas shopping. For the moment it didn't matter that their coats were unfashionable and the cuffs of their acrylic sweaters protruded lumpishly from the outgrown sleeves or that their frozen feet were beginning to smart, in the anticipation of chilblains, in their scuffed shoes in reaction to the heater under the seat. They were alone in the compartment except for a youth with a personal stereo leaking a tinny rhythm through the headphones.

With their heavy greenish-blonde hair cut straight across their foreheads and lying flat as lasagne over the hoods and shoulders of their school duffles, and their green eyes set wide apart in the flat planes of their pale faces, despite Stella's borrowed fishnet stockings which were causing her much *angst*, they looked younger than their fourteen and twelve years. It would not have occurred to either of them that anybody staring at them might have been struck by anything other than their horrible clothes. Their desire, thwarted by Him and by lack of money of their own, was to look like everybody else. The dog hairs that adhered so stubbornly to the navy-blue cloth and bristled starkly in the harsh and electric light of the winter morning were from Barney, the black and white border collie, grown fat and snappish in his old age, who bared his teeth at his new master, the usurper, and slunk into a corner at his homecoming, as the girls slunk into their bedroom.

'It's cruel to keep that animal alive,' He would say. 'What's it got to live for? Smelly old hearthrug.'

And while He discoursed on the Quality of Life, running a finger down Mummy's spine or throat, Barney's legs would splay out worse than they usually did and his claws click louder on the floor, or a malodorous cloud of stagnant pond water emanate from his coat. It was a sign of His power that Barney was thus diminished.

'We'll know when the Time has come. And the Time has not yet come,' said Mummy with more energy than she summoned to champion her elder daughters, while Barney rolled a filmy blue eye in her direction. The dog, despite his shedding coat, was beyond reproach as far as the girls were concerned; his rough back and neck had been salted with many tears, and he was their one link with their old life, before their father had disappeared and before their mother had defected to the enemy.

'What are you going to buy Him?' Vanessa asked.

'Nothing. I'm making His present.'

'What?' Vanessa was incredulous, fearing treachery afoot.

'I'm knitting Him a pair of socks. Out of stinging nettles.'

'I wish I could knit.' After a wistful pause she started to say, 'I wonder what He would . . .'

'I'm placing a total embargo on His name today,' Stella cut her off. 'Don't speak of Him. Don't even think about Him. Right, Regan?'

'Right, Goneril. Why does He call us those names?'

'They're the Ugly Sisters in Cinderella of course.'

'I thought they were called Anastasia and . . . and . . .'

'Embargo,' said Stella firmly.

'It's not Cordelia who needs a fairy godmother, it's us. Wouldn't it be lovely if one day . . .'

'Grow up.'

So that was how He saw them, bewigged and garishly rouged, two pantomime dames with grotesque beauty spots and fishnet tights stretched over their bandy men's calves, capering jealously round Cordelia's high chair. Cordelia herself, like Barney, was adored unreservedly, but after her birth, with one hand rocking the transparent hospital cot in which she lay, as a joke which they could not share, He had addressed her half-sisters as Goneril and Regan. Their mother had protested then, but now sometimes she used the names. Under His rule, comfortable familiar objects vanished and routines were abolished. Exposed to His mockery, they became ludicrous. One example was the Bunnykins china they ate from sometimes, not in a wish to prolong their babyhood but because it was there. All the pretty mismatched bits and pieces of crockery were superseded by a stark white service from Habitat and there were new forks with vicious prongs and knives which cut. Besotted with Cordelia's dimples and black curls, He lost all patience with his stepdaughters, with their tendency to melancholy and easily provoked tears which their pink eyelids and noses could not conceal, and like a vivisector with an electric prod tormenting two albino mice, he discovered all their most vulnerable places.

Gypsies had travelled up in the train earlier, making their buttonholes and nosegays, and had left the seats and floor strewn with a litter of twigs and petals and scraps of silver foil like confetti.

'We might see Princess Di or Fergie,' Vanessa said, scuffing the debris with her foot. 'They do their Christmas shopping in Harrods.'

'The Duchess of York to you. Oh yes, we're sure to run into them. Anyway, Princess Diana does her shopping in Covent Garden.'

'Well then!' concluded Vanessa triumphantly. She noticed the intimation of a cold sore on her sister's superior lip and was for a second glad. Harrods and Covent Garden were where they had decided, last night, after lengthy discussions, to go, their excited voices rising from guarded whispers to a normal pitch, until He had roared upstairs at them to shut up. Vanessa's desire to go to Hamleys had been overruled. She had cherished a secret craving for a tube of plastic stuff with which you blew bubbles and whose petroleum smell she found as addictive as the smell of new Elastoplast. Now she took out her purse and checked her ticket and counted her money yet again. Even with the change she had filched fearfully from the trousers He had left sprawled across the bedroom chair, it didn't amount to much. Stella was rich, as the result of her paper round and the tips she had received in return for the cards she had put through her customers' doors wishing them a 'Merry Christmas from your Newsboy/Newsgirl', with a space for her to sign her name. She would have been even wealthier had He not demanded the money for the repair of the iron whose flex had burst into flames in her hand while she was ironing His shirt. She could not see how it had been her fault but supposed it must have been. The compartment filled up at each stop and the girls stared out of the window rather than speak in public, or look at each other and see mirrored in her sister her own unsatisfactory self.

The concourse at Victoria was scented with sweet and sickening melted chocolate from a booth that sold fresh-baked cookies, and crowded with people criss-crossing each other with loaded trolleys, running to hurl themselves at the barriers, dragging luggage and children; queuing help-lessly for tickets while the minutes to departure ticked away, swirling round the bright scarves outside the Tie Rack, panic-buying festive socks and glittery bow ties, slurping coffee and beer and champing croissants and pizzas and jacket potatoes and trying on earrings. It had changed so much from the last time they had seen it that only the late arrival of their train and the notice of cancellation and delay on the indicator board reassured them that they were at the right Victoria Station.

'I've got to go to the Ladies.'

'OK.'

Vanessa attempted to join the dismayingly long queue trailing down the stairs but Stella had other plans.

'Stell-a! Where are you going?'

She dragged Vanessa into the side entrance of the Grosvenor Hotel.

'Stella, we can't! It's a HOTEL! We'll be ARRESTED . . .' She wailed as Stella's fingers pinched through her coat sleeves, propelling her up the steps and through the glass doors.

'Shut up. Look as though we're meeting somebody.'

Vanessa could scarcely breathe as they crossed the foyer, expecting at any moment a heavy hand to descend on her shoulder, a liveried body to challenge them, a peaked cap to thrust into their faces. The thick carpet accused their feet. Safely inside the Ladies, she collapsed against a basin.

'Well? Isn't this better than queuing for hours? And it's free.'

'Supposing someone comes?'

'Oh stop bleating. It's perfectly all right. Daddy brought me here once – no one takes any notice of you.'

The door opened and the girls fled into cubicles and locked the doors. After what seemed like half an hour Vanessa slid back the bolt and peeped round the door. There was Stella, bold as brass, standing at the mirror between the sleek backs of two women in stolen fur coats applying a stub of lipstick to her mouth. She washed and dried her hands and joined Stella, meeting a changed face in the glass: Stella's eyelids were smudged with green and purple, her lashes longer and darker, her skin matt with powder.

'Where did you get it?' she whispered hoarsely as the two women moved away.

'Tracy' – the friend who had lent her the stockings, with whom Vanessa, until they were safely on the train, had feared Stella would choose to go Christmas shopping instead of with her.

Women came and went and Vanessa's fear was forgotten as she applied the cosmetics to her own face.

'Now we look a bit more human,' said Stella as they surveyed themselves, Goneril and Regan, whom their own father had named Star and Butterfly.

Vanessa Cardui, Painted Lady, sucked hollows into her cheeks and said, 'We really need some blusher, but it can't be helped.'

'Just a sec.'

'But Stella, it's a bar . . . we can't . . .!'

Her alarm flooded back as Stella marched towards Edward's Bar.

'We'll get drunk. What about our shopping?'

Ignoring the animated temperance tract clutching her sleeve, Stella scanned the drinkers.

'Looking for someone, Miss?' the barman asked pleasantly.

'He's not here yet,' said Stella. 'Come on, Vanessa.'

She checked the coffee lounge on the way out, and as they recrossed the fearful foyer it dawned on Vanessa that Stella had planned this all along; all the way up in the train she had been expecting to find Daddy in Edward's Bar. That had been the whole point of the expedition.

She was afraid that Stella would turn like an injured dog and snap at her. She swallowed hard, her heart racing, as if there were words that would make everything all right, if only she could find them.

'What?' Stella did turn on her.

'He might be in Harrods.'

'Oh yes. Doing his Christmas shopping with Fergie and Di. Buying our presents.'

Vanessa might have retorted, 'The Duchess of York to you,' but she knew better than to risk the cold salt wave of misery between them engulfing the whole day. A gypsy woman barred their way with a sprig of foliage wrapped in silver.

'Lucky white heather. Bring you luck.'

'Doesn't seem to have brought you much,' snarled Stella pushing past her.

'You shouldn't have been so rude. Now she'll put a curse on us,' wailed Vanessa.

'It wasn't even real heather, dumbell.'

'Now there's no chance we'll meet Daddy.'

Stella strode blindly past the gauntlet of people rattling

tins for The Blind. Vanessa dropped in a coin and hurried
after her down the steps. As they went to consult the map
of the Underground they almost stumbled over a man
curled up asleep on the floor, a bundle of grey rags and
hair and beard tied up with string. His feet, black with
dirt and disease, protruded shockingly bare into the path
of the Christmas shoppers. The sisters stared, their faces
chalky under their make-up.

Then a burst of laughter and singing broke out. A group
of men and women waving bottles and cans were holding
a private crazed party, dancing in their disfigured clothes
and plastic accoutrements; a woman with long grey hair
swirling out in horizontal streamers from a circlet of tinsel
was clasping a young man in a close embrace as they
shuffled round ringing 'All I want for Christmas is my two
front teeth', and he threw back his head to 'pour the last
drops from a bottle into a toothless black hole, while their
companions beat out a percussion accompaniment on
bottles and cans with a braying brass of hiccups. They
were the only people in that desperate and shoving
crowded place who looked happy.

Stella and Vanessa were unhappy as they travelled
down the escalator. The old man's feet clawed at them
with broken and corroded nails; the revellers, although
quite oblivious to the citizens of the other world, had
frightened them; the gypsy's curse hung over them.

Harrods was horrendous. They moved bemused through
the silken scented air, buffeted by headscarves, furs and
green shopping bags. Fur and feathers in the Food Hall
left them stupefied in the splendour of death and beauty
and money.

'This is crazy,' said Stella. 'We probably couldn't afford
even one quail's egg.'

Mirrors flung their scruffy reflections back at them and
they half-expected to be shown the door by one of the green
and gold guards and after an hour of fingering and coveting
and temptation they were out in the artic wind of Knights-
bridge with two packs of Christmas cards and a round gold
box of chocolate Napoleons.

* * *

In Covent Garden they caught the tail end of a piece of street theatre as a green spotted pantomime cow curvetted at them with embarrassing udders, swiping the awkward smiles off their faces with its tail. A woman dressed as a clown bopped them on the head with a balloon and thrust a bashed-in hat at them. Close to she looked fierce rather than funny. The girls paid up. It seemed that everybody in the city was engaged in a conspiracy to make them hand over their money. Two hot chocolates made another serious inroad in their finances, the size of the bill souring the floating islands of cream as they sat on white wrought-iron chairs sipping from long spoons to the accompaniment of a young man busking on a violin backed by a stereo system.

'You should've brought your cello,' said Vanessa and choked on her chocolate as she realized she could hardly have said anything more tactless. It was He who had caused Stella's impromptu resignation from the school orchestra, leaving it in the lurch. His repetition, in front of two of His friends, of an attributed reprimand by Sir Thomas Beecham to a lady cellist had made it impossible for her to practise at home and unthinkable that she should perform on a public platform to an audience sniggering like Him, debasing her and the music.

'It's – it's not my kind of music,' she had lied miserably to Miss Philips, the music teacher.

'Well, Stella, I must say I had never thought of *you* as a disco queen,' Miss Philips had said bitterly.

Her hurt eyes strobed Stella's pale selfish face and falling-down socks as she wilted against the wall. Accusations of letting down her fellow musicians followed, and reminders of Miss Philips's struggle to obtain the cello from another school, her own budget and resources being so limited. She ignored Stella in the corridor thereafter and the pain of this was still with her, like the ominous ache in her lower abdomen. She wished she was at home curled up with a hot-water bottle.

'Bastard,' she said. 'Of all the gin joints in all the suburbs of south-east London, why did He have to walk into ours?' Mummy had brought Him home from a rehearsal of the amateur production of *Oklahoma* for which she was doing the costumes, ostensibly for an emergency fitting of His

Judd Fry outfit, the trousers and boots of which were presenting difficulties. The girls had almost clapped the palms off their hands after the mournful rendition of 'Poor Judd is Dead'. It would always be a show-stopper for them.

Stella wished she had had one of the cards from Harrods to put in the school postbox for Miss Philips, but she hadn't, and now it was too late. Vanessa bought a silver heart-shaped balloon for Cordelia, or, as Stella suspected, for herself. They wandered round the stalls and shops over the slippery cobblestones glazed with drizzle.

'How come, whichever way we go, we always end up in Central Avenue?' Vanessa wondered.

Stella gave up the pretence that she knew exactly where she was going. 'It'll be getting dark soon. We must buy *something*.'

They battled their way into the Convent Garden General Store and joined the wet and unhappy throng desperate to spend money they couldn't afford on presents for people who would not want what they received, to the relentless musical threat that Santa Claus was coming to town. 'If this is more fun than just shopping,' said Stella as they queued to pay for their doubtful purchases, quoting from the notice displayed over the festive and jokey goods, 'I think I prefer just shopping. Sainsbury's on Saturday morning is paradise compared to this.'

Stella was seduced by a gold mesh star and some baubles as fragile and iridescent as soap bubbles, to hang on the conifer in the corner of the bare front room, decked in scrawny tinsel too sparse for its sprawling branches and topped with the fairy with a scorch mark in her greying crêpe-paper skirt where it had once caught in a candle. The candles, with most of their old decorations, had been vetoed by Him and had been replaced by a set of fairy lights with more twisted emerald green flex than bulbs in evidence.

'I wish we hadn't got a tree,' Vanessa said.

'I know. Cordelia likes it, though.'

'I suppose so. That's all that matters really. I mean, Christmas *is* for kids, isn't it?'

Vanessa showed her the bubble bath disguised as a bottle of gin which she was buying for Him.

'Perhaps He'll drink it.'

'Early on Christmas morning, nursing a savage hang-over, He rips open His presents and desperate for a hair-of-the-dog He puts the bottle to his lips. Bubbles come out of His nose and mouth, He falls to the floor – '

'Screaming in agony.'

' – screaming in agony, foaming at the mouth. The heroic efforts of his distraught stepdaughters fail to revive him. An ambulance is called but it gets stuck in traffic. When they finally reach the hospital all the nurses are singing carols in the wards and no one can find the stomach pump. A doctor in a paper hat tells the sorrowing sisters – or are they laughing, who can tell? – that it's too late. He has fallen victim to His own greed. How much does it cost?'

'Two pounds seventy-nine.'

'Cheap at twice the price.'

After leaving the shop they collided with a superstructure formed by two supermarket trolleys lashed together and heaped with a perilous pyramid of old clothes and plastic bags and utensils and bits of hardware like taps and broken car exhausts and hub-caps, the handlebars of a bicycle fronting it like antlers and three plumes of pampas grass waving in dirty Prince of Wales feathers. The owner was dragging a large cardboard box from beneath a stall of skirts and blouses.

'What do you think he wants that box for?' Vanessa wondered.

'To sleep in, of course. He probably lives in Cardboard City.'

'Cardboard City?'

'It's where the homeless people live. They all sleep in cardboard boxes underneath the Arches.'

'What arches?'

'*The* Arches, of course. Shall we go home now?'

Vanessa nodded. They were wet and cold, and the rain had removed most of their make-up, saving them the trouble of doing it themselves before they encountered Him. The feet of Stella's stockings felt like muddy string in her leaking shoes.

* * *

They were huddled on the packed escalator, two drowned rats going up to Victoria, when Vanessa screamed shrilly.

'Daddy!'

She pointed to a man on the opposing escalator.

'It's Daddy, quick Stella, we've got to get off.' She would have climbed over the rail if Stella hadn't held her.

'It's not him.'

'It is. It is. *Daddy!*'

Faces turned to stare. The man turned and their eyes met as they were carried upwards and he was borne inexorably down. Vanessa tried to turn to run down against the flow of the escalator but she was wedged. The man was gone for ever.

'It wasn't him, I tell you.' Stella fought the sobbing Vanessa at the top of the stair, they were yelling at each other in the mêlée of commuters and shoppers. She succeeded in dragging her through the barrier, still crying, 'It was him. Now we'll never see him again.'

'Daddy hasn't got a beard, you know that. And he'd never wear a balaclava. Come *on*, Vanessa, we'll miss our train.'

'It was him. Let's go back, please, please.'

'Look, stupid, that guy was a down and out. A vagrant. A wino. A meths drinker. It couldn't possibly have been Daddy.'

On the home-bound train Stella carefully opened the box of chocolate Napoleons. There were so many that nobody would notice if a couple were missing. She took out two gold coins and sealed the box again. For the rest of their lives Vanessa would be convinced that she had seen her father, and Stella would never be sure. The chocolate dissolved in their mouths as they crossed the Thames.

'Where is Cardboard City?' whispered Vanessa. 'How do you get there?'

'"Follow the Yellow Brick Road . . ."'

The silver heart-shaped balloon floated on its vertical string above the heads and newspapers of the passengers.

'"Now I know I've got a heart, because it's breaking."'

'It's just a slow puncture,' Stella said. She stuck a gift label on to the balloon's puckering silver skin. It ruined the look of it, but it was kindly meant. Vanessa looked out of the window at the moon melting like a lemon drop in the freezing sky above the chimney tops of Clapham and pictured it shining on the cold frail walls and pinnacles of Cardboard City.

'I don't want Daddy to sleep in a cardboard box,' she said.

'It's a great life,' Stella said savagely. 'Didn't you see those people singing and dancing?'

Paule Marshall

Paule Marshall was born in Brooklyn, New York in 1929. Her parents emigrated from Barbados during the First World War and she grew up in Brooklyn during the Depression. She graduated in English Literature from Brooklyn College in 1953 and went on to edit a Black journal, *Our World*. She has taught creative writing at many American universities. She has a son and lives in New York.

As a child Paule Marshall would listen to her mother's friends from Barbados as they sat around the table in the basement of her Brooklyn brownstone home. She loved to listen to their West Indian dialect and expressive talk, and used this for inspiration in much of her writing. Works she has published include the novels *Brown Girl Brownstones* (1959), *Praisesong for the Widow* (1983) and the collection of stories *Merle and Other Stories* (1985) from which the following story is taken.

'To Daduh, In Memoriam' arises out of a visit Paule Marshall made when she was nine to her grandmother (whose nickname was Daduh) on the island of Barbados. During the year she spent with her grandmother there was a power struggle going on between them. She writes, 'It was as if we both knew at a level beyond words that I had come into the world not only to love her and continue her line, but to take her very life in order that I might live.' The story explores the conflicts and rivalries between the child of the city and her proud old grandmother.

To Da-Duh, in Memoriam
Paule Marshall

'... Oh Nana! all of you is not involved in this evil
business Death,
Nor all of us in life.'
– From 'At My Grandmother's Grave,' by Lebert Bethune

I did not see her at first I remember. For not only was it
dark inside the crowded disembarkation shed in spite of
the daylight flooding in from outside, but standing there
waiting for her with my mother and sister I was still
somewhat blinded from the sheen of tropical sunlight on
the water of the bay which we had just crossed in the
landing boat, leaving behind us the ship that had brought
us from New York lying in the offing. Besides, being only
nine years of age at the time and knowing nothing of
islands I was busy attending to the alien sights and sounds
of Barbados, the unfamiliar smells.

I did not see her, but I was alerted to her approach by
my mother's hand which suddenly tightened around mine,
and looking up I traced her gaze through the gloom in the
shed until I finally made out the small, purposeful, painfully erect figure of the old woman headed our way.

Her face was drowned in the shadow of an ugly rolled-
brim brown felt hat, but the details of her slight body and
of the struggle taking place within it were clear enough –
an intense, unrelenting struggle between her back which
was beginning to bend ever so slightly under the weight of
her eighty-odd years and the rest of her which sought to
deny those years and hold that back straight, keep it in
line. Moving swiftly toward us (so swiftly it seemed she
did not intend stopping when she reached us but would
sweep past us out the doorway which opened onto the sea

and like Christ walk upon the water!), she was caught
between the sunlight at her end of the building and the
darkness inside – and for a moment she appeared to
contain them both: the light in the long severe old-
fashioned white dress she wore which brought the sense of
a past that was still alive into our bustling present and in
the snatch of white at her eye; the darkness in her black
high-top shoes and in her face which was visible now that
she was closer.

It was as stark and fleshless as a death mask, that face.
The maggots might have already done their work, leaving
only the framework of bone beneath the ruined skin and
deep wells at the temple and jaw. But her eyes were alive,
unnervingly so for one so old, with a sharp light that
flicked out of the dim clouded depths like a lizard's tongue
to snap up all in her view. Those eyes betrayed a child's
curiosity about the world, and I wondered vaguely seeing
them, and seeing the way the bodice of her ancient dress
had collapsed in on her flat chest (what had happened to
her breasts?), whether she might not be some kind of child
at the same time that she was a woman, with fourteen
children, my mother included, to prove it. Perhaps she was
both, both child and woman, darkness and light, past and
present, life and death – all the opposites contained and
reconciled in her.

'My Da-duh,' my mother said formally and stepped
forward. The name sounded like thunder fading softly in
the distance.

'Child,' Da-duh said, and her tone, her quick scrutiny of
my mother, the brief embrace in which they appeared to
shy from each other rather than touch, wiped out the
fifteen years my mother had been away and restored the
old relationship. My mother, who was such a formidable
figure in my eyes, had suddenly with a word been reduced
to my status.

'Yes, God is good,' Da-duh said with a nod that was like
a tic. 'He has spared me to see my child again.'

We were led forward then, apologetically because not
only did Da-duh prefer boys but she also liked her grandchildren to be 'white,' that is, fair-skinned; and we had, I
was to discover, a number of cousins, the outside children

of white estate managers and the like, who qualified. We, though, were as black as she.

My sister being the oldest was presented first. 'This one takes after the father,' my mother said and waited to be reproved.

Frowning, Da-duh tilted my sister's face toward the light. But her frown soon gave way to a grudging smile, for my sister with her large mild eyes and little broad winged nose, with our father's high-cheeked Barbadian cast to her face, was pretty.

'She's goin' be lucky,' Da-duh said and patted her once on the cheek. 'Any girl child that takes after the father does be lucky.'

She turned then to me. But oddly enough she did not touch me. Instead leaning close, she peered hard at me, and then quickly drew back. I thought I saw her hand start up as though to shield her eyes. It was almost as if she saw not only me, a thin truculent child who it was said took after no one but myself, but something in me which for some reason she found disturbing, even threatening. We looked silently at each other for a long time there in the noisy shed, our gaze locked. She was the first to look away.

'But Adry,' she said to my mother and her laugh was cracked, thin, apprehensive. 'Where did you get this one here with this fierce look?'

'We don't know where she came out of, my Da-duh,' my mother said, laughing also. Even I smiled to myself. After all I had won the encounter. Da-duh had recognized my small strength – and this was all I ever asked of the adults in my life then.

'Come, soul,' Da-duh said and took my hand. 'You must be one of those New York terrors you hear so much about.'

She led us, me at her side and my sister and mother behind, out of the shed into the sunlight that was like a bright driving summer rain and over to a group of people clustered beside a decrepit lorry. They were our relatives, most of them from St Andrews although Da-duh herself lived in St Thomas, the women wearing bright print dresses, the colors vivid against their darkness, the men rusty black suits that encased them like strait-jackets. Da-duh, holding fast to my hand, became my anchor as they circled round us like a nervous sea, exclaiming, touching us with their calloused hands, embracing us shyly. They laughed in awed bursts: 'But look Adry got big-big children!' / 'And see the nice things they wearing, wrist watch and all!' / 'I tell you, Adry has done all right for sheself in New York . . .'

Da-duh, ashamed at their wonder, embarrassed for them, admonished them the while. 'But oh Christ,' she said, 'why you all got to get on like you never saw people from "Away" before? You would think New York is the only place in the world to hear wunna. That's why I don't like to go anyplace with you St Andrews people, you know. You all ain't been colonized.'

We were in the back of the lorry finally, packed in among the barrels of ham, flour, cornmeal and rice and the trunks of clothes that my mother had brought as gifts. We made our way slowly through Bridgetown's clogged streets, part of a funereal procession of cars and open-sided buses, bicycles and donkey carts. The dim little limestone shops and offices along the way marched with us, at the same mournful pace, toward the same grave ceremony – as did the people, the women balancing huge baskets on top their heads as if they were no more than hats they wore to shade them from the sun. Looking over the edge of the lorry I watched as their feet slurred the dust. I listened, and their voices, raw and loud and dissonant in the heat, seemed to be grappling with each other high overhead.

Da-duh sat on a trunk in our midst, a monarch amid her court. She still held my hand, but it was different now. I had suddenly become her anchor, for I felt her fear of the lorry with its asthmatic motor (a fear and distrust, I later learned, she held of all machines) beating like a pulse in her rough palm.

As soon as we left Bridgetown behind though, she relaxed, and while the others around us talked she gazed at the canes standing tall on either side of the winding marl road. 'C'dear,' she said softly to herself after a time. 'The canes this side are pretty enough.'

They were too much for me. I thought of them as giant weeds that had overrun the island, leaving scarcely any room for the small tottering houses of sunbleached pine we passed or the people, dark streaks as our lorry hurtled by. I suddenly feared that we were journeying, unaware that we were, toward some dangerous place where the canes, grown as high and thick as a forest, would close in on us and run us through with their stiletto blades. I longed then for the familiar: for the street in Brooklyn where I lived, for my father who had refused to accompany us ('Blowing out good money on foolishness,' he had said of the trip), for a game of tag with my friends under the chestnut tree outside our aging brownstone house.

'Yes, but wait till you see St. Thomas canes,' Da-duh was saying to me. 'They's canes father, bo,' she gave a proud arrogant nod. 'Tomorrow, God willing, I goin' take you out in the ground and show them to you.'

True to her word Da-duh took me with her the following day out into the ground. It was a fairly large plot adjoining her weathered board and shingle house and consisting of a small orchard, a good-sized canepiece and behind the canes, where the land sloped abruptly down, a gully. She had purchased it with Panama money sent her by her eldest son, my uncle Joseph, who had died working on the canal. We entered the ground along a trail no wider than her body and as devious and complex as her reasons for showing me her land. Da-duh strode briskly ahead, her slight form filled out this morning by the layers of sacking petticoats she wore under her working dress to protect her against the damp. A fresh white cloth, elaborately arranged around her head, added to her height, and lent her a vain, almost roguish air.

Her pace slowed once we reached the orchard, and glancing back at me occasionally over her shoulder, she pointed out the various trees.

'This here is a breadfruit,' she said. 'That one yonder is a pawpaw. Here's a guava. This is a mango. I know you don't have anything like these in New York. Here's a sugar apple.' (The fruit looked more like artichokes than apples to me.) 'This one bears limes . . .' She went on for some time, intoning the names of the trees as though they were those of her gods. Finally, turning to me, she said, 'I know you don't have anything this nice where you come from.'

Then, as I hesitated: 'I said I know you don't have anything this nice where you come from . . .'

'No,' I said and my world did seem suddenly lacking.

Da-duh nodded and passed on. The orchard ended and we were on the narrow cart road that led through the canepiece, the canes clashing like swords above my cowering head. Again she turned and her thin muscular arms spread wide, her dim gaze embracing the small field of canes, she said – and her voice almost broke under the weight of her pride, 'Tell me, have you got anything like these in that place where you were born?'

'No.'

'I din' think so. I bet you don't even know that these canes here and the sugar you eat is one and the same thing. That they does throw the canes into some damn machine at the factory and squeeze out all the little life in them to make sugar for you all so in New York to eat. I bet you don't know that.'

'I've got two cavities and I'm not allowed to eat a lot of sugar.'

But Da-duh didn't hear me. She had turned with an inexplicably angry motion and was making her way rapidly out of the canes and down the slope at the edge of the field which led to the gully below. Following her apprehensively down the incline amid a stand of banana plants whose leaves flapped like elephants ears in the wind, I found myself in the middle of a small tropical wood – a place dense and damp and gloomy and tremulous with the fitful play of light and shadow as the leaves high above moved against the sun that was almost hidden from view. It was a violent place, the tangled foliage fighting each other for a chance at the sunlight, the branches of the trees locked in what seemed an immemorial struggle, one both necessary and inevitable. But despite the violence, it was pleasant, almost peaceful in the gully, and beneath the thick undergrowth the earth smelled like spring.

This time Da-duh didn't even bother to ask her usual question, but simply turned and waited for me to speak.

'No,' I said, my head bowed. 'We don't have anything like this in New York.'

'Ah,' she cried, her triumph complete. 'I din' think so.

Why, I've heard that's a place where you can walk till you near drop and never see a tree.'

'We've got a chestnut tree in front of our house,' I said.

'Does it bear?' She waited. 'I ask you, does it bear?'

'Not anymore,' I muttered. 'It used to, but not anymore.'

She gave the nod that was like a nervous twitch. 'You see,' she said. 'Nothing can bear there.' Then, secure behind her scorn, she added, 'But tell me, what's this snow like that you hear so much about?'

Looking up, I studied her closely, sensing my chance, and then I told her, describing at length and with as much drama as I could summon not only what snow in the city was like, but what it would be like here, in her perennial summer kingdom.

'... And you see all these trees you got here,' I said. 'Well, they'd be bare. No leaves, no fruit, nothing. They'd be covered in snow. You see your canes. They'd be buried under tons of snow. The snow would be higher than your head, higher than your house, and you wouldn't be able to come down into this here gully because it would be snowed under ...'

She searched my face for the lie, still scornful but intrigued. 'What a thing, huh?' she said finally, whispering it softly to herself.

'And when it snows you couldn't dress like you are now,' I said. 'Oh no, you'd freeze to death. You'd have to wear a hat and gloves and galoshes and ear muffs so your ears wouldn't freeze and drop off, and a heavy coat. I've got a Shirley Temple coat with fur on the collar. I can dance. You wanna see?'

Before she could answer I began, with a dance called the Truck which was popular back then in the 1930s. My right forefinger waving, I trucked around the nearby trees and around Da-duh's awed and rigid form. After the Truck I did the Suzy-Q, my lean hips swishing, my sneakers sidling zigzag over the ground. 'I can sing,' I said and did so, starting with 'I'm Gonna Sit Right Down and Write Myself a Letter,' then without pausing, 'Tea For Two,' and ending with 'I Found a Million Dollar Baby in a Five and Ten Cent Store.'

For long moments afterwards Da-duh stared at me as if

I were a creature from Mars, an emissary from some world she did not know but which intrigued her and whose power she both felt and feared. Yet something about my performance must have pleased her, because bending down she slowly lifted her long skirt and then, one by one, the layers of petticoats until she came to a drawstring purse dangling at the end of a long strip of cloth tied round her waist. Opening the purse she handed me a penny. 'Here,' she said half-smiling against her will. 'Take this to buy yourself a sweet at the shop up the road. There's nothing to be done with you, soul.'

From then on, whenever I wasn't taken to visit relatives, I accompanied Da-duh out into the ground, and alone with her amid the canes or down in the gully I told her about New York. It always began with some slighting remark on her part: 'I know they don't have anything this nice where you come from,' or 'Tell me, I hear those foolish people in New York does do such and such ...' But as I answered, recreating my towering world of steel and concrete and machines for her, building the city out of words, I would feel her give way. I came to know the signs of her surrender: the total stillness that would come over her little hard dry form, the probing gaze that like a surgeon's knife sought to cut through my skull to get at the images there, to see if I were lying; above all, her fear, a fear nameless and profound, the same one I had felt beating in the palm of her hand that day in the lorry.

Over the weeks I told her about refrigerators, radios, gas stoves, elevators, trolley cars, wringer washing machines, movies, airplanes, the cyclone at Coney Island, subways, toasters, electric lights: 'At night, see, all you have to do is flip this little switch on the wall and all the lights in the house go on. Just like that. Like magic. It's like turning on the sun at night.'

'But tell me,' she said to me once with a faint mocking smile, 'do the white people have all these things too or it's only the people looking like us?'

I laughed. 'What d'ya mean,' I said. 'The white people have even better.' Then: 'I beat up a white girl in my class last term.'

'Beating up white people!' Her tone was incredulous.

'How you mean!' I said, using an expression of hers. 'She called me a name.'

For some reason Da-duh could not quite get over this and repeated in the same hushed, shocked voice, 'Beating up white people now! Oh, the lord, the world's changing up so I can scarce recognize it anymore.'

One morning toward the end of our stay, Da-duh led me into a part of the gully that we had never visited before, an area darker and more thickly overgrown than the rest, almost impenetrable. There in a small clearing amid the dense bush, she stopped before an incredibly tall royal palm which rose cleanly out of the ground, and drawing the eye up with it, soared high above the trees around it into the sky. It appeared to be touching the blue dome of sky, to be flaunting its dark crown of fronds right in the blinding white face of the late morning sun.

Da-duh watched me a long time before she spoke, and then she said, very quietly, 'All right, now, tell me if you've got anything this tall in that place you're from.'

I almost wished, seeing her face, that I could have said no. 'Yes,' I said. 'We've got buildings hundreds of times this tall in New York. There's one called the Empire State building that's the tallest in the world. My class visited it last year and I went all the way to the top. It's got over a hundred floors. I can't describe how tall it is. Wait a minute. What's the name of that hill I went to visit the other day, where they have the police station?'

'You mean Bissex?'

'Yes, Bissex. Well, the Empire State Building is way taller than that.'

'You're lying now!' she shouted, trembling with rage. Her hand lifted to strike me.

'No, I'm not,' I said. 'It really is, if you don't believe me I'll send you a picture postcard of it soon as I get back home so you can see for yourself. But it's way taller than Bissex.'

All the fight went out of her at that. The hand poised to strike me fell limp to her side, and as she stared at me, seeing not me but the building that was taller than the highest hill she knew, the small stubborn light in her eyes (it was the same amber as the flame in the kerosene lamp she lit at dusk) began to fail. Finally, with a vague gesture that even in the midst of her defeat still tried to dismiss me and my world, she turned and started back through the gully, walking slowly, her steps groping and uncertain, as if she were suddenly no longer sure of the way, while I followed triumphant yet strangely saddened behind.

The next morning I found her dressed for our morning walk but stretched out on the Berbice chair in the tiny drawing room where she sometimes napped during the afternoon heat, her face turned to the window beside her. She appeared thinner and suddenly indescribably old.

'My Da-duh,' I said.

'Yes, nuh,' she said. Her voice was listless and the face she slowly turned my way was, now that I think back on it, like a Benin mask, the features drawn and almost distorted by an ancient abstract sorrow.

'Don't you feel well?' I asked.

'Girl, I don't know.'

'My Da-duh, I goin' boil you some bush tea,' my aunt, Da-duh's youngest child, who lived with her, called from the shed roof kitchen.

'Who tell you I need bush tea?' she cried, her voice assuming for a moment its old authority. 'You can't even rest nowadays without some malicious person looking for you to be dead. Come girl,' she motioned me to a place beside her on the old-fashioned lounge chair, 'give us a tune.'

I sang for her until breakfast at eleven, all my brash irreverent Tin Pan Alley songs, and then just before noon we went out into the ground. But it was a short, dispirited walk. Da-duh didn't even notice that the mangoes were beginning to ripen and would have to be picked before the village boys got to them. And when she paused occasionally and looked out across the canes or up at her trees it wasn't as if she were seeing them but something else. Some huge, monolithic shape had imposed itself, it seemed, between her and the land, obstructing her vision. Returning to the house she slept the entire afternoon on the Berbice chair.

She remained like this until we left, languishing away the mornings on the chair at the window gazing out at the land as if it were already doomed; then, at noon, taking the brief stroll with me through the ground during which she seldom spoke, and afterwards returning home to sleep till almost dusk sometimes.

On the day of our departure she put on the austere, ankle length white dress, the black shoes and brown felt hat (her town clothes she called them), but she did not go with us to town. She saw us off on the road outside her house and in the midst of my mother's tearful protracted farewell, she leaned down and whispered in my ear, 'Girl, you're not to forget now to send me the picture of that building, you hear.'

By the time I mailed her the large colored picture postcard of the Empire State building she was dead. She died during the famous '37 strike which began shortly after we left. On the day of her death England sent planes flying low over the island in a show of force – so low, according to my aunt's letter, that the downdraft from them shook the ripened mangoes from the trees in Da-duh's orchard. Frightened, everyone in the village fled into the canes. Except Da-duh. She remained in the house at the window so my aunt said, watching as the planes came swooping and screaming like monstrous birds down over the village, over her house, rattling her trees and flattening the young canes in her field. It must have seemed to her lying there that they did not intend pulling out of their dive, but like the hard-back beetles which hurled themselves with suicidal force against the walls of the house at night, those menacing silver shapes would hurl themselves in an ecstasy of self-immolation onto the land, destroying it utterly.

When the planes finally left and the villagers returned they found her dead on the Berbice chair at the window.

She died and I lived, but always, to this day even, within the shadow of her death. For a brief period after I was grown I went to live alone, like one doing penance, in a loft above a noisy factory in downtown New York and there painted seas of sugar-cane and huge swirling Van Gogh suns and palm trees striding like brightly-plumed Tutsi warriors across a tropical landscape, while the thunderous tread of the machines downstairs jarred the floor beneath my easel, mocking my efforts.

Kate Chopin

Kate Chopin was born in 1854, the child of an Irish immigrant father and a French mother from St Louis, USA. Her father died in a train crash when she was very young and she was brought up in an all female household – mother, grandmother and great grandmother, in the American South.

From the time of her marriage in 1870 Kate Chopin lived in New Orleans. She read widely, and she especially admired the stories of the French writer Guy de Maupassant, translating a number of his pieces for American publication.

Chopin's own writing began after the death of her husband in 1883. She took her work seriously, bravely picking up and extending themes which less confident writers had tended to pass over. She was especially keen to explore the complex experiences of women in relation to men, family life and the wider world. Her writing was often controversial and many of her stories were refused publication during her lifetime. However, her focus on women's experience and the accessibility of her writing style has generated a lot of recent interest in her work. Chopin's short novel *The Awakening* (1899) is now regularly in print, as are several collections of her short stories. Kate Chopin died in 1904.

'The Story of an Hour', written in 1894, originally for a magazine readership, is an excellent example of a Kate Chopin short story. Although over a hundred years old, its theme is just as relevant today; and its direct, almost cinematic style, coupled with an unexpected narrative twist, opens it to a range of fascinating interpretations.

The Story of an Hour
Kate Chopin

Knowing that Mrs Mallard was afflicted with a heart trouble, great care was taken to break to her as gently as possible the news of her husband's death.

It was her sister Josephine who told her, in broken sentences; veiled hints that revealed in half concealing. Her husband's friend Richards was there, too, near her. It was he who had been in the newspaper office when intelligence of the railroad disaster was received, with Brently Mallard's name leading the list of 'killed.' He had only taken the time to assure himself of its truth by a second telegram, and had hastened to forestall any less careful, less tender friend in bearing the sad message.

She did not hear the story as many women have heard the same, with a paralyzed inability to accept its significance. She wept at once, with sudden, wild abandonment, in her sister's arms. When the storm of grief had spent itself she went away to her room alone. She would have no one follow her.

There stood, facing the open window, a comfortable, roomy armchair. Into this she sank, pressed down by a physical exhaustion that haunted her body and seemed to reach into her soul.

She could see in the open square before her house the tops of trees that were all aquiver with the new spring life. The delicious breath of rain was in the air. In the street below a peddler was crying his wares. The notes of a distant song which some one was singing reached her faintly, and countless sparrows were twittering in the eaves.

There were patches of blue sky showing here and there

through the clouds that had met and piled one above the other in the west facing her window.

She sat with her head thrown back upon the cushion of the chair, quite motionless, except when a sob came up into her throat and shook her, as a child who has cried itself to sleep continues to sob in its dreams.

She was young, with a fair, calm face, whose lines bespoke repression and even a certain strength. But now there was a dull stare in her eyes, whose gaze was fixed away off yonder on one of those patches of blue sky. It was not a glance of reflection, but rather indicated a suspension of intelligent thought.

There was something coming to her and she was waiting for it, fearfully. What was it? She did not know; it was too subtle and elusive to name. But she felt it, creeping out of the sky, reaching toward her through the sounds, the scents, the color that filled the air.

Now her bosom rose and fell tumultuously. She was beginning to recognize this thing that was approaching to possess her, and she was striving to beat it back with her will – as powerless as her two white slender hands would have been.

When she abandoned herself a little whispered word escaped her slightly parted lips. She said it over and over under her breath: 'free, free, free!' The vacant stare and the look of terror that had followed it went from her eyes. They stayed keen and bright. Her pulses beat fast, and the coursing blood warmed and relaxed every inch of her body.

She did not stop to ask if it were or were not a monstrous joy that held her. A clear and exalted perception enabled her to dismiss the suggestion as trivial.

She knew that she would weep again when she saw the kind, tender hands folded in death; the face that had never looked save with love upon her, fixed and gray and dead. But she saw beyond that bitter moment a long procession of years to come that would belong to her absolutely. And she opened and spread her arms out to them in welcome.

There would be no one to live for her during those coming years; she would live for herself. There would be no powerful will bending hers in that blind persistence with which men and women believe they have a right to impose a private will upon a fellow-creature. A kind intention or a cruel intention made the act seem no less a crime as she looked upon it in that brief moment of illumination.

And yet she had loved him – sometimes. Often she had not. What did it matter! What could love, the unsolved mystery, count for in face of this possession of self-assertion which she suddenly recognized as the strongest impulse of her being!

'Free! Body and soul free!' she kept whispering.

Josephine was kneeling before the closed door with her lips to the keyhole, imploring for admission. 'Louise, open the door! I beg; open the door – you will make yourself ill. What are you doing, Louise? For heaven's sake open the door.'

'Go away. I am not making myself ill.' No; she was drinking in a very elixir of life through that open window.

Her fancy was running riot along those days ahead of her. Spring days, and summer days, and all sorts of days that would be her own. She breathed a quick prayer that life might be long. It was only yesterday she had thought with a shudder that life might be long.

She arose at length and opened the door to her sister's importunities. There was a feverish triumph in her eyes, and she carried herself unwittingly like a goddess of Victory. She clasped her sister's waist, and together they descended the stairs. Richards stood waiting for them at the bottom.

Some one was opening the front door with a latchkey. It was Brently Mallard who entered, a little travel-stained, composedly carrying his grip-sack and umbrella. He had been far from the scene of the accident, and did not even know there had been one. He stood amazed at Josephine's piercing cry; at Richards' quick motion to screen him from the view of his wife.

But Richards was too late.

When the doctors came they said she had died of heart disease – of joy that kills.

Marjorie Barnard

Marjorie Barnard was born in Sydney, Australia in 1897. She graduated from Sydney University in 1918 and was offered a scholarship to study in England. Her father prevented her from accepting the scholarship, and in 1920 she began work as a librarian. In the same year she published a collection of stories for children, *The Ivory Gate*, and began her literary collaboration with her friend Flora Eldershaw. Between 1929 and 1947 they published five novels, three historical works and one of the first collections of essays on Australian literature. They published their work under the joint pseudonym of Marjorie Barnard Eldershaw.

'The Lottery' is a story published under Marjorie Barnard's own name in a collection called *The Persimmon Tree*. The themes of the stories in this collection, first published in 1943, have remained topical, and the collection was republished by Virago in 1985. As well as being a novelist, and short story writer for children and adults, Marjorie Barnard wrote biographies and historical works, including *A History of Australia*. She died in 1987.

The Lottery
Majorie Barnard

The first that Ted Bilborough knew of his wife's good fortune was when one of his friends, an elderly wag, shook his hand with mock gravity and murmured a few words of manly but inappropriate sympathy. Ted didn't know what to make of it. He had just stepped from the stairway on to the upper deck of the 6.15 p.m. ferry from town. Fred Lewis seemed to have been waiting for him, and as he looked about he got the impression of newspapers and grins and a little flutter of half derisive excitement, all focussed on himself. Everything seemed to bulge towards him. It must be some sort of leg pull. He felt his assurance threatened, and the corner of his mouth twitched uncomfortably in his fat cheek, as he tried to assume a hard boiled manner.

'Keep the change, laddie,' he said.

'He doesn't know, actually he doesn't know.'

'Your wife's won the lottery!'

'He won't believe you. Show him the paper. There it is as plain as my nose. Mrs Grace Bilborough, 52 Cuthbert Street.' A thick, stained forefinger pointed to the words. 'First prize, £5000 Last Hope Sydicate.'

'He's taking it very hard,' said Fred Lewis, shaking his head.

They began thumping him on the back. He had travelled on that ferry every week-day for the last ten years, barring a fortnight's holiday in January, and he knew nearly everyone. Even those he didn't know entered into the spirit of it. Ted filled his pipe nonchalantly but with unsteady fingers. He was keeping that odd unsteadyness, that seemed to begin somewhere deep in his chest, to himself. It was a wonder that fellows in the office hadn't got hold of

this, but they had been busy today in the hot loft under
the chromium pipes of the pneumatic system, sending
down change and checking up on credit accounts. Sale
time. Grace might have let him know. She could have rung
up from Thompson's. Bill was always borrowing the lawn
mower and the step ladder, so it would hardly be asking a
favour in the circumstances. But that was Grace all over.

'If I can't have it myself, you're the man I like to see get
it.'

They meant it too. Everyone liked Ted in a kind sort of
way. He was a good fellow in both senses of the word. Not
namby pamby, always ready for a joke but a good citizen
too, a good husband and father. He wasn't the sort that
refused to wheel the perambulator. He flourished the
perambulator. His wife could hold up her head, they payed
their bills weekly and he even put something away, not
much but something, and that was a triumph the way
things were, the ten per cent knocked off his salary in the
depression not restored yet, and one thing and another.
And always cheerful, with a joke for everyone. All this was
vaguely present in Ted's mind. He'd always expected in a
trusting sort of way to be rewarded, but not through Grace.

'What are you going to do with it, Ted?'

'You won't see him for a week, he's going on a jag.' This
was very funny because Ted never did, not even on Anzac
Day.

A voice with a grievance said, not for the first time, 'I've
had shares in a ticket every week since it started, and I've
never won a cent.' No one was interested.

'You'll be going off for a trip somewhere?'

'They'll make you president of the Tennis Club and you'll
have to donate a silver cup.'

They were flattering him underneath the jokes.

'I expect Mrs Bilborough will want to put some of it away
for the children's future,' he said. It was almost as if he
were giving an interview to the press, and he was pleased
with himself for saying the right thing. He always referred
to Grace in public as Mrs Bilborough. He had too nice a
social sense to say 'the Missus.'

Ted let them talk, and looked out of the window. He
wasn't interested in the news in the paper tonight. The

little boat vibrated fussily, and left a long wake like
moulded glass in the quiet river. The evening was drawing
in. The sun was sinking into a bank of grey cloud, soft and
formless as mist. The air was dusky, so that its light was
closed into itself and it was easy to look at, a thick golden
disc more like a moon rising through smoke than the sun.
It threw a single column of orange light on the river, the
ripples from the ferry fanned out into it, and their tiny
shadows truncated it. The bank, rising steeply from the
river and closing it in till it looked like a lake, was already
bloomed with shadows. The shapes of two churches and a
broken frieze of pine trees stood out against the gentle sky,
not sharply, with a soft arresting grace. The slopes, wooded
and scattered with houses, with dim and sunk in idyllic
peace. The river showed thinly bright against the dark
lane. Ted could see that the smooth water was really a
pale tawny gold with patches, roughened by the turning
tide, of frosty blue. It was only when you stared at it and
concentrated your attention that you realised the colours.
Turning to look down stream away from the sunset, the
water gleamed silvery grey with dark clear scrabblings
upon it. There were two worlds, one looking towards the
sunset with the dark land against it dreaming and still,
and the other looking down stream over the silvery river
to the other bank, on which all the light concentrated.
Houses with windows of orange fire, black trees, a great
silver gasometer, white oil tanks with the look of clumsy
mushrooms, buildings serrating the sky, even a suggestion
seen or imagined of red roofs, showing up miraculously in
that airy light.

'Five thousand pounds,' he thought. 'Five thousand
pounds.' Five thousand pounds at five per cent, five thousand pounds stewing gently away in its interest, making
old age safe. He could do almost anything he could think
of with five thousand pounds. It gave his mind a stretched
sort of feeling, just thinking of it. It was hard to connect
five thousand pounds with Grace. She might have let him
know. And where had the five and threepence to buy the
ticket come from? He couldn't help wondering about that.
When you budgeted as carefully as they did there wasn't
five and threepence over. If there had been, well, it

wouldn't have been over at all, he would have put it in the
bank. He hadn't noticed any difference in the housekeeping, and he prided himself he noticed everything. Surely
she hadn't been running up bills to buy lottery tickets. His
mind darted here and there suspiciously. There was something secretive in Grace, and he'd thought she told him
everything. He'd taken it for granted, only, of course, in
the ordinary run there was nothing to tell. He consciously
relaxed the knot in his mind. After all, Grace had won the
five thousand pounds. He remembered charitably that she
had always been a good wife to him. As he thought that he
had a vision of the patch on his shirt, his newly washed
cream trousers laid out for tennis, the children's neatness,
the tidy house. That was being a good wife. And he had
been a good husband, always brought his money home and
never looked at another woman. Theirs was a model home,
everyone acknowledged it, but – well – somehow he found
it easier to be cheerful in other people's homes than his
own. It was Grace's fault. She wasn't cheery and easy
going. Something moody about her now. Woody. He'd worn
better than Grace, anyone could see that, and yet it was
he who had had the hard time. All she had to do was to
stay at home and look after the house and the children.
Nothing much in that. She always seemed to be working,
but he couldn't see what there was to do that could take
her so long. Just a touch of woman's perversity. It wasn't
that Grace had aged. Ten years married and with two
children, there was still something girlish about her – raw,
hard girlishness that had never mellowed. Grace was –
Grace, for better or for worse. Maybe she'd be a bit brighter
now. He could not help wondering how she had managed
the five and three. If she could shower five and threes
about like that, he'd been giving her too much of the
housekeeping. And why did she want to give it that
damnfool name 'Last Hope.' That meant there had been
others, didn't it? It probably didn't mean a thing, just a
lucky tag.

A girl on the seat opposite was sewing lace on silkies for
her trousseau, working intently in the bad light.

'Another one starting out,' Ted thought.

'What about it?' said the man beside him.

Ted hadn't been listening.

The ferry had tied up at his landing stage and Ted got off. He tried not to show in his walk that his wife had won £5000. He felt jaunty and tired at once. He walked up the hill with a bunch of other men, his neighbours. They were still teasing him about the money, they didn't know how to stop. It was a very still, warm evening. As the sun descended into the misty bank on the horizon it picked out the delicate shapes of clouds invisibly sunk in the mass, outlining them with a fine thread of gold.

One by one the men dropped out, turning into side streets or opening garden gates till Ted was alone with a single companion, a man who lived in a semi-detached cottage at the end of the street. They were suddenly very quiet and sober. Ted felt the ache round his mouth where he'd been smiling and smiling.

'I'm awfully glad you've had this bit of luck.'

'I'm sure you are, Eric,' Ted answered in a subdued voice.

'There's nobody I'd sooner see have it.'

'That's very decent of you.'

'I mean it.'

'Well, well, I wasn't looking for it.'

'We could do with a bit of luck like that in our house.'

'I bet you could.'

'There's an instalment on the house due next month, and Nellie's got to come home again. Seems as if we'd hardly done paying for the wedding.'

'That's bad.'

'She's expecting, so I suppose Mum and Dad will be let in for all that too.'

'It seems only the other day Nellie was a kid getting round on a scooter.'

'They grow up,' Eric agreed. 'It's the instalment that's the rub. First of next month. They expect it on the nail too. If we hadn't that hanging over us it wouldn't matter about Nellie coming home. She's our girl, and it'll be nice to have her about the place again.'

'You'll be as proud as a cow with two tails when you're a grandpa.'

'I suppose so.'

They stood mutely by Eric's gate. An idea began to

flicker in Ted's mind, and with it a feeling of sweetness and happiness and power such as he had never expected to feel.

'I won't see you stuck, old man,' he said.

'That's awfully decent of you.'

'I mean it.'

They shook hands as they parted. Ted had only a few steps more and he took them slowly. Very warm and dry, he thought. The garden will need watering. Now he was at his gate. There was no one in sight. He stood for a moment looking about him. It was as if he saw the house he had lived in for ten years, for the first time. He saw that it had a mean, narrow-chested appearance. The roof tiles were discoloured, the woodwork needed painting, the crazy pavement that he had laid with such zeal had an unpleasant flirtatious look. The revolutionary thought formed in his mind. 'We might leave here.' Measured against the possibilities that lay before him, it looked small and mean. Even the name, 'Emoh Ruo,' seemed wrong, pokey.

Ted was reluctant to go in. It was so long since anything of the least importance had happened between him and Grace, that it made him shy. He did not know how she would take it. Would she be in a dither and no dinner ready? He hoped so but feared not.

He went into the hall, hung up his hat and shouted in a big bluff voice. 'Well, well, well, and where's my rich wife?'

Grace was in the kitchen dishing dinner.

'You're late,' she said. 'The dinner's spoiling.'

The children were quiet but restless, anxious to leave the table and go out to play. 'I got rid of the reporters,' Grace said in a flat voice. Grace had character, trust her to handle a couple of cub reporters. She didn't seem to want to talk about it to her husband either. He felt himself, his voice, his stature dwindling. He looked at her with hard eyes. 'Where did she get the money,' he wondered again, but more sharply.

Presently they were alone. There was a pause. Grace began to clear the table. Ted felt that he must do something. He took her awkwardly into his arms. 'Grace, aren't you pleased?'

She stared at him a second then her face seemed to fall together, a sort of spasm, something worse than tears. But she twitched away from him. 'Yes,' she said, picking up a pile of crockery and making for the kitchen. He followed her.

'You're a dark horse, never telling me a word about it.'

'She's like a Red Indian,' he thought. She moved about the kitchen with quick nervous movments. After a moment she answered what was in his mind:

'I sold my mother's ring and chain. A man came to the door buying old gold. I bought a ticket every week till the money was gone.'

'Oh,' he said. Grace had sold her mother's wedding ring to buy a lottery ticket.

'It was my money.'

'I didn't say it wasn't.'

'No, you didn't.'

The plates clattered in her hands. She was evidently feeling something, and feeling it strongly. But Ted didn't know what. He couldn't make her out.

She came and stood in front of him, her back to the littered table, her whole body taut. 'I suppose you're wondering what I am going to do? I'll tell you. I'm going away. By myself. Before it's too late. I'm going tomorrow.'

He didn't seem to be taking it in.

'Beattie will come and look after you and the children. She'll be glad to. It won't cost you a penny more than it does now,' she added.

He stood staring at her, his flaccid hands hanging down, his face sagging.

'Then you meant what you said in the paper. "Last Hope?"' he said.

'Yes,' she answered.

Joyce Carol Oates

Joyce Carol Oates was born in Millersport, New York in 1938. She studied English at Syracuse and Wisconsin Universities and has been a Professor of English for most of her life. She married Raymond Smith in 1961.

She is a prolific writer and has published more than sixteen novels since her first *With Shuddering Fall* in 1964. Other novels include *Do With Me What You Will* (1973) and *Angel of Light* (1981). In addition she has published poems, plays, criticism and a large number of short story collections, including 'The Poisoned Kiss' (1975) and 'Nightside' (1977), from which 'Fatal Woman' is taken.

From such a vast body of work it is difficult to pin down any particular approach, however she often writes about extraordinary people who are single-minded and who desire to dominate life. These people want everything and everyone to fit in with their ideas, sometimes with disastrous consequences. Oates likes to enter the lives of her characters imaginatively – from Pentecostal preachers to children in the slum of Detroit. Her stories often deal with violent incidents, forcing the reader to confront some uncomfortable truths.

In 'Fatal Woman' we meet a woman who is obsessed with the idea of her own attractiveness and the power she supposes she has over men. As we read her thoughts we begin to question her version of what has happened in her life.

Fatal Woman
Joyce Carol Oates

The first, the very first time, I became aware of my power over men, I was only twelve years old.

I remember distinctly. Because that was the year of the terrible fire downtown, the old Tate Hotel, where eleven people were burned to death and there was such scandal. The hotel owner was charged with negligence and there was a trial and a lot of excitement. Anyway, I was walking downtown with one of my girl friends, Holly Turnbull, and there was a boardwalk or something by the hotel, which was just a ruin, what was left of it, and you could smell the smoke, such an ugly smell, and I was looking at the burnt building and I said to Holly: 'My God do you smell *that?*' Thinking it was burnt flesh. I swear it was. But Holly pulled my arm and said 'Peggy, there's somebody watching us!'

Well, this man was maybe my father's age. He was just standing there a few yards away, watching me. He wore a dark suit, a white shirt, but no tie. His face was wrinkled on one side, he was squinting at me so hard his left eye was almost closed. You'd think he was going to smile or say something funny, grimacing like that. But no. He just stared. Stared and stared and stared. His lips moved but I couldn't hear what he said – it was just a mumble. It wasn't meant for me to hear.

My hair came to my waist. It was light brown, always shiny and well-brushed. I had nice skin: no blemishes. Big brown eyes. A pretty mouth. Figure just starting to be what it is today. I didn't know it, but that man was the first, the very first, to look at me in that special way.

He scared me, though. He smelled like something black

and scorched and ugly. Holly and I both ran away giggling,
and didn't look back.

As I grew older my attractiveness to men increased and
sometimes I almost wished I was an elderly woman! – free
at last from the eyes and the winks and the whistles and
the remarks and sometimes even the nudges. But that
won't be for a while, so I suppose I must live with it.
Sometimes I want to laugh, it seems so silly. It seems so
crazy. I study myself in the mirror from all angles and I'm
not being modest when I say that, in my opinion, I don't
seem that much prettier than many women I know. Yet
I've been in the presence of these women and it always
happens if a man or a boy comes along he just skims over
the others and when he notices me he stares. There must
be something about me, an aura of some kind, that I don't
know about.

Only a man would know.

I got so exasperated once, I asked: What it is? Why are
you bothering *me*? But it came out more or less
humorously.

Gerry Swanson was the first man who really dedicated
himself to me – didn't just ogle me or whistle or make
fresh remarks – but really fell in love and followed me
around and ignored his friends' teasing. He walked by our
house and stood across the street, waiting, just for a
glimpse of me, and he kept meeting me by accident
downtown or outside the high school no matter if I was
with my girl friends and they all giggled like crazy at the
sight of him. Poor Gerry Swanson, everybody laughed. I
blushed so, I couldn't help it. It made me happy that he
was in love with me, but it frightened me too, because
he was out of school a few years and seemed a lot older
than the boys I knew. (I had a number of boy friends in
high school – I didn't want to limit myself to just one. I
was very popular; it interfered with my schoolwork to some
extent, but I didn't care. For instance, I was the lead in the
Spring Play when I was only a sophomore, and I was on
the cheerleading squad for three years, and I was First
Maid-in-Waiting to the Senior Queen. I wasn't voted
Senior Queen because, as my boy friends said, all the girls
were jealous of me and deliberately voted against me, but

all the boys voted for me. I didn't exactly believe them. I
think some of the girls probably voted for me – I had lots
of friends – and naturally some of the boys would have
voted for other candidates. That's only realistic.) When
Gerry came along, I was sixteen. He was working for his
father's construction company and I was surprised he
would like a girl still in high school, but he did; he
telephoned all the time and took me out, on Sundays
mainly, to the matinée downtown, because my father didn't
trust him, and he tried to buy me things, and wrote letters,
and made such a fool of himself everybody laughed at him,
and I couldn't help laughing myself. I asked him once what
it was: *Why* did he love me so much?

He just swallowed and stared at me and couldn't say a
word.

As I've grown older this attractiveness has gradually
increased, and in recent weeks it has become something of
a nuisance. Maybe I dress provocatively – I don't know.
Certainly I don't amble about with my bare midriff showing and legs bare up to the buttocks, like many other girls,
and I've recently had my hair cut quite short, for the warm
weather. I have noticed, though, that my navy-blue dress
seems to attract mention; possibly it fits my body too
tightly. I don't know. I wish certain men would just ignore
me. For instance, a black man on the street the other day
– a black *police*man, who should know better – was staring
at me from behind his sunglasses with the boldest look you
could imagine. It was shocking. It was really rude. I gave
him a cold look and kept right on walking, but I was
trembling inside. Later, I wondered if maybe I should have
pretended not to notice. I wondered if he might think I had
snubbed him because of the colour of his skin – but that
had nothing to do with it, not a thing! I'm not prejudiced
in any way and never have been.

At the hospital there are young attendants, college-age
boys, at the very time of life when they are most suscep-
tible to visual stimulation; they can't help noticing me, and
staring and staring. When I took the elevator on Monday
to the tenth floor, where Harold's room is, one of the
attendants hurried to get on with me. The elevator was
empty except for us two. The boy blushed so his face went

beet-red. I tried to make things casual by remarking on the weather and the pretty petunias out front by the sidewalk, but the boy was too nervous and he didn't say a word until the door opened on the tenth floor and I stepped out. 'You're so beautiful!' – he said. But I just stepped out and pretended not to hear and walked down the corridor.

Eddie telephoned the other evening, Wednesday. He asked about Harold and I told him everything I knew, but then he didn't say goodbye, he just kept chattering and chattering – then he asked suddenly if he could come over to see me. That very night. His voice quavered and I was just so shocked! – but I should have seen it coming over the years. I should have seen it coming. I told him it was too late, I was going to bed, but could he please put my daughter on the phone for a minute? That seemed to subdue him.

In church I have noticed our minister watching me, sometimes out of the corner of his eye, as he gives his sermon. He is a few years younger than I am, and really should know better. But I've had this certain effect all my life – when I'm sitting in an audience and there are men addressing the group. I first noticed it, of course, in junior and senior high school, but it didn't seem to be so powerful then. Maybe I wasn't so attractive then. It's always the same: the man addressing us looks around the room, smiling, talking more or less to everyone, and then his eye happens to touch upon me and his expression changes abruptly and sometimes he even loses the thread of what he is saying, and stammers, and has to repeat himself. After that he keeps staring helplessly at me and addresses his words only to me, as if the rest of the audience didn't exist. It's the strangest thing ... If I take pity on him I can somehow 'release' him, and allow him to look away and talk to the others; it's hard to explain how I do this – I give a nearly imperceptible nod and a little smile and I *will* him to be released, and it works, and the poor man is free.

I take pity on men, most of the time.

Sometimes I've been a little daring, I admit it. A little flirtatious. Once at Mirror Lake there were some young Italian men on the beach, and Harold saw them looking at me, and heard one of them whistle, and there was an unpleasant scene ... Harold said I encouraged them by the way I walked. I don't know: I just don't know. It seems a woman's body sometimes might be flirtatious by itself, without the woman herself exactly knowing.

The telephone rang tonight and when I picked up the receiver no one answered.

'Eddie,' I said, 'is this Eddie? I know it's you, dear, and you shouldn't do this – you know better – what if Barbara finds out, or one of the children? My daughter would be heartbroken to know her own husband is making telephone calls like this – You know better, dear!'

He didn't say a word, but he didn't hang up. I was the one to break the connection.

When I turned off the lights downstairs just now, and checked the windows, and checked the doors to make sure they were locked, I peeked out from behind the living-room shade and I could see someone standing across the street, on the sidewalk. It was that black policeman! But he wasn't in his uniform. I don't think he was in his uniform. He's out there right now, standing there, waiting, watching this house. Just like Gerry Swanson used to.

I'm starting to get frightened.

Everyone tells me to be strong, not to break down – about Harold, they mean; about the way the operation turned out. Isn't it a pity? they say. But he's had a full life, a rich life. You've been married how long – ? Happily married. Of course. And your children, and the grandchildren. 'A full, rich life.' And they look at me with that stupid pity, never seeing me, not *me*, never understanding anything. What do I have to do with an old man, I want to scream at them. What do I have to do with an old dying man?

One of them stood on the sidewalk that day, staring at me. No, it was on a boardwalk. The air stank with something heavy and queer and dark. I giggled, I ran away and never looked back. Now one of them is outside the house at this very moment. He's waiting, watching for me. If I move the blind, he will see me. If I snap on the light and raise the blind even a few inches, he will see me. What has he to do with that old man in the hospital, what have

I to do with that old man ...? But I can't help being frightened.

For the first time in my life I wonder – what is going to happen?

Doris Lessing

Doris Lessing was born to British parents in Iran in 1919. At the age of five she was taken to live on a lonely farm in southern Rhodesia, later called Zimbabwe. She began writing while young and read widely to educate herself. She attended a convent school until the age of fourteen, when she left to work as an au pair, and later as a secretary.

From a young age Doris Lessing had a hatred for the unjust system of government in Rhodesia; she was very involved in political activities in pursuit of racial equality. Her second marriage, in 1945, was to Gottfried Lessing, a German Jewish communist who was in exile in Africa. In 1949 they moved to England with their son.

Doris Lessing brought the manuscript of her first novel with her to England, and it was published in 1950 under the title *The Grass is Singing*. A series of four related novels (published between 1952 and 1969) collectively called *Children of Violence*, follows the life of the heroine Martha Quest who moves from Africa to England. In the late 1960s Doris Lessing moved away from her commitment to socialism and became interested in mystical Sufism. Her novels reflected this interest, and between 1979 and 1985 she wrote a five-volume fantasy series called *Canopus in Argos: Archives*. In the early 1980s Lessing experimented with using the pseudonym Jane Somers to see if the novels of an apparently unknown writer would still be published; they were. Recent novels have been published under her own name, and have dealt with morally complex situations.

Doris Lessing's work is varied and prolific. She has published several collections of short stories including: *A Man and Two Women* (1965) and *The Story of a Non-Marrying Man and other stories* (1972), 'An Old Woman and her Cat' comes from the later collection.

An Old Woman and Her Cat

Doris Lessing

Her name was Hetty, and she was born with the twentieth century. She was seventy when she died of cold and malnutrition. She had been alone for a long time, since her husband had died of pneumonia in a bad winter soon after the Second World War. He had not been more than middle-aged. Her four children were now middle-aged, with grown children. Of these descendants one daughter sent her Christmas cards, but otherwise she did not exist for them. For they were all respectable people, with homes and good jobs and cars. And Hetty was not respectable. She had always been a bit strange, these people said, when mentioning her at all.

When Fred Pennefather, her husband, was alive, and the children just growing up, they all lived much too close and uncomfortable in a Council flat in that part of London which is like an estuary, with tides of people flooding in and out: they were not half a mile from the great stations of Euston, St Pancras and King's Cross. The blocks of flats were pioneers in that area, standing up grim, grey, hideous, among many acres of little houses and gardens, all soon to be demolished so that they could be replaced by more tall grey blocks. The Pennefathers were good tenants, paying their rent, keeping out of debt; he was a building worker, 'steady', and proud of it. There was no evidence then of Hetty's future dislocation from the normal, unless it was that she very often slipped down for an hour or so to the platforms where the locomotives drew in and ground out again. She liked the smell of it all, she said. She liked to see people moving about, 'coming and going from all those foreign places'. She meant Scotland, Ireland, the North of England. These visits into the din, the smoke, the massed swirling people, were for her a drug, like other people's drinking or gambling. Her husband teased her, calling her a gipsy. She was in fact part-gipsy, for her mother had been one, but had chosen to leave her people and marry a man who lived in a house. Fred Pennefather liked his wife for being different from the run of the women he knew, and had married her because of it; but her children were fearful that her gipsy blood might show itself in worse ways than haunting railway stations. She was a tall women with a lot of glossy black hair, a skin that tanned easily, and dark strong eyes. She wore bright colours, and enjoyed quick tempers and sudden reconciliations. In her prime she attracted attention, was proud and handsome. All this made it inevitable that the people in those streets should refer to her as 'that gipsy woman'. When she heard them, she shouted back that she was none the worse for that.

After her husband died and the children married and left, the Council moved her to a small flat in the same building. She got a job selling food in a local store, but found it boring. There seem to be traditional occupations for middle-aged women living alone, the busy and responsible part of their lives being over. Drink. Gambling. Looking for another husband. A wistful affair or two. That's about it. Hetty went through a period of, as it were, testing out all these, like hobbies, but tired of them. While still earning her small wage as a saleswoman, she began a trade in buying and selling second-hand clothes. She did not have a shop of her own, but bought or begged clothes from householders, and sold these to stalls and the secondhand shops. She adored doing this. It was a passion. She gave up her respectable job and forgot all about her love of trains and travellers. Her room was always full of bright bits of cloth, a dress that had a pattern she fancied and did not want to sell, strips of beading, old furs, embroidery, lace. There were street traders among the people in the flats, but there was something in the way Hetty went about it that lost her friends. Neighbours of twenty or thirty years' standing said she had gone queer, and wished to know her no longer. But she did not mind. She was enjoying herself too much, particularly the moving about the streets with her old perambulator, in which she crammed what she was buying or selling. She liked the gossiping, the bargaining, the wheedling from householders. It was this last which – and she knew this quite well of course – the neighbours objected to. It was the thin edge of the wedge. It was begging. Decent people did not beg. She was no longer decent.

Lonely in her tiny flat, she was there as little as possible, always preferring the lively streets. But she had after all to spend some time in her room, and one day she saw a kitten lost and trembling in a dirty corner, and brought it home to the block of flats. She was on a fifth floor. While the kitten was growing into a large strong tom, he ranged about that conglomeration of staircases and lifts and many dozens of flats, as if the building were a town. Pets were not actively persecuted by the authorities, only forbidden and then tolerated. Hetty's life from the coming of the cat became more sociable, for the beast was always making friends with somebody in the cliff that was the block of flats across the court, or not coming home for nights at a time so that she had to go and look for him and knock on doors and ask, or returning home kicked and limping, or bleeding after a fight with his kind. She made scenes with the kickers, or the owners of the enemy cats, exchanged cat lore with cat-lovers, was always having to bandage and nurse her poor Tibby. The cat was soon a scarred warrior with fleas, a torn ear, and a ragged look to him. He was a multicoloured cat and his eyes were small and yellow. He was a long way down the scale from the delicately coloured, elegantly shaped pedigree cats. But he was independent, and often caught himself pigeons when he could no longer stand the tinned cat food, or the bread and packet gravy Hetty fed him, and he purred and nestled when she grabbed him to her bosom at those times she suffered loneliness. This happened less and less. Once she had realized that her children were hoping that she would leave them alone because the old rag-trader was an embarrassment to them, she accepted it, and a bitterness that always had wild humour in it welled up only at times like Christmas. She sang or chanted to the cat: 'You nasty old beast, filthy old cat, nobody wants you, do they Tibby, no, you're just an alley tom, just an old stealing cat, hey Tibs, Tibs, Tibs.'

The building teemed with cats. There were even a couple of dogs. They all fought up and down the grey cement corridors. There were sometimes dog and cat messes which someone had to clear up, but which might be left for days and weeks as part of neighbourly wars and feuds. There were many complaints. Finally an official came from the Council to say that the ruling about keeping animals was going to be enforced. Hetty, like the others, would have to have her cat destroyed. This crisis coincided with a time of bad luck for her. She had had flu; had not been able to earn money; had found it hard to get out for her pension; had run into debt. She owed a lot of back rent, too. A television set she had hired and was not paying for attracted the visit of a television representative. The neighbours were gossiping that Hetty had 'gone savage'. This was because the cat had brought up the stairs and along the passageways a pigeon he had caught, shedding feathers and blood all the way; a woman coming in to complain found Hetty plucking the pigeon to stew it, as she had done with others, sharing the meal with Tibby.

'You're filthy,' she would say to him, setting the stew down to cool in his dish. 'Filthy old thing. Eating that dirty old pigeon. What do you think you are, a wild cat? Decent cats don't eat dirty birds. Only those old gipsies eat wild birds.'

One night she begged help from a neighbour who had a car, and put into the car herself, the television set, the cat, bundles of clothes, and the pram. She was driven across London to a room in a street that was a slum because it was waiting to be done up. The neighbour made a second trip to bring her bed and her mattress, which were tied to the roof of the car, a chest of drawers, an old trunk, saucepans. It was in this way that she left the street in which she had lived for thirty years, nearly half her life.

She set up house again in one room. She was frightened to go near 'them' to re-establish pension rights and her identity, because of the arrears of rent she had left behind, and because of the stolen television set. She started trading again, and the little room was soon spread, like her

last, with a rainbow of colours and textures and lace and
sequins. She cooked on a single gas ring and washed in the
sink. There was no hot water unless it was boiled in
saucepans. There were several old ladies and a family of
five children in the house, which was condemned.

She was in the ground-floor back, with a window which
opened on to a derelict garden, and her cat was happy in a
hunting ground that was a mile around this house where
his mistress was so splendidly living. A canal ran close by,
and in the dirty city-water were islands which a cat could
reach by leaping from moored boat to boat. On the islands
were rats and birds. There were pavements full of fat
London pigeons. The cat was a fine hunter. He soon had
his place in the hierarchies of the local cat population and
did not have to fight much to keep it. He was a strong male
cat, and fathered many litters of kittens.

In that place Hetty and he lived five happy years. She
was trading well, for there were rich people close by to
shed what the poor needed to buy cheaply. She was not
lonely, for she made a quarrelling but satisfying friendship
with a woman on the top floor, a widow like herself who
did not see her children either. Hetty was sharp with the
five children, complaining about their noise and mess, but
she slipped them bits of money and sweets after telling
their mother that 'she was a fool to put herself out for
them, because they wouldn't appreciate it.' She was living
well, even without her pension. She sold the television set
and gave herself and her friend upstairs some day-trips to
the coast, and bought a small radio. She never read books
or magazines. The truth was that she could not write or
read, or only so badly it was no pleasure to her. Her cat
was all reward and no cost, for he fed himself, and
continued to bring in pigeons for her to cook and eat, for
which in return he claimed milk.

'Greedy Tibby, you greedy *thing*, don't think I don't
know, oh yes I do, you'll get sick eating those old pigeons,
I do keep telling you that, don't I?'

At last the street was being done up. No longer a
uniform, long, disgraceful slum, houses were being bought
by the middle-class people. While this meant more good
warm clothes for trading – or begging, for she still could

not resist the attraction of getting something for nothing by the use of her plaintive inventive tongue, her still flashing handsome eyes – Hetty knew, like her neighbours, that soon this house with its cargo of poor people would be bought for improvement.

In the week Hetty was seventy years old, came the notice that was the end of this little community. They had four weeks to find somewhere else to live.

Usually, the shortage of housing being what it is in London – and everywhere else in the world, of course – these people would have had to scatter, fending for themselves. But the fate of this particular street was attracting attention, because a municipal election was pending. Homelessness among the poor was finding a focus in this street which was a perfect symbol of the whole area, and indeed the whole city, half of it being fine, converted, tasteful houses, full of people who spent a lot of money, and half being dying houses tenanted by people like Hetty.

As a result of speeches by councillors and churchmen, local authorities found themselves unable to ignore the victims of this redevelopment. The people in the house Hetty was in were visited by a team consisting of an unemployment officer, a social worker and a rehousing officer. Hetty, a strong gaunt old woman wearing a scarlet wool suit she had found among her cast-offs that week, a black knitted tea-cosy on her head, and black buttoned Edwardian boots too big for her, so that she had to shuffle, invited them into her room. But although all were well used to the extremes of poverty, none wished to enter the place, but stood in the doorway and made her this offer: that she should be aided to get her pension – why had she not claimed it long ago? – and that she, together with the four other old ladies in the house should move to a Home run by the Council out in the northern suburbs. All these women were used to, and enjoyed, lively London, and while they had no alternative but to agree, they fell into a saddened and sullen state. Hetty agreed too. The last two winters had set her bones aching badly, and a cough was never far away. And while perhaps she was more of an urban soul even than the others, since she had walked up and down so many streets with her old perambulator

loaded with rags and laces, and since she knew so inti-
mately London's texture and taste, she minded least of all
the idea of a new home 'among green fields'. There were,
in fact, no fields near the promised Home, but for some
reason all the old ladies had chosen to bring out this old
song of a phrase, as if it belonged to their situation, that of
old women not far off death. 'It will be nice to be near
green fields again,' they said to each other over cups of tea.

The housing officer came to make final arrangements.
Hetty Pennefather was to move with the others in two
weeks' time. The young man, sitting on the very edge of
the only chair in the crammed room, because it was greasy
and he suspected it had fleas or worse in it, breathed as
lightly as he could because of the appalling stink: there
was a lavatory in the house, but it had been out of order
for three days, and it was just the other side of a thin wall.
The whole house smelled.

The young man, who knew only too well the extent of
the misery due to lack of housing, who knew how many old
people abandoned by their children did not get the offer to
spend their days being looked after by the authorities,
could not help feeling that this wreck of a human being
could count herself lucky to get a place in this Home, even
if it was – and he knew and deplored the fact – an
institution in which the old were treated like naughty and
dim-witted children until they had the good fortune to die.

But just as he was telling Hetty that a van would be
coming to take her effects and those of the other four old
ladies, and that she need not take anything more with her
than her clothes 'and perhaps a few photographs', he saw
what he had thought was a heap of multicoloured rags get
up and put its ragged gingery-black paws on the old
woman's skirt. Which today was a cretonne curtain covered
with pink and red roses that Hetty had pinned around her
because she liked the pattern.

'You can't take that cat with you,' he said automatically.
It was something he had to say often, and knowing what
misery the statement caused, he usually softened it down.
But he had been taken by surprise.

Tibby now looked like a mass of old wool that has been
matting together in dust and rain. One eye was perma-

nently half-closed, because a muscle had been ripped in a fight. One ear was vestigial. And down a flank was a hairless slope with a thick scar on it. A cat-hating man had treated Tibby as he treated all cats, to a pellet from his airgun. The resulting wound had taken two years to heal. And Tibby smelled.

No worse, however, than his mistress, who sat stiffly still, bright-eyed with suspicion, hostile, watching the well-brushed, tidy young man from the Council.

'How old is that beast?'

'Ten years, no, only eight years, he's a young cat about five years old,' said Hetty, desperate.

'It looks as if you'd do him a favour to put him out of his misery,' said the young man.

When the official left, Hetty had agreed to everything. She was the only one of the old women with a cat. The others had budgerigars or nothing. Budgies were allowed in the Home.

She made her plans, confided in the others, and when the van came for them and their clothes and photographs and budgies, she was not there, and they told lies for her. 'Oh, we don't know where she can have gone, dear,' the old women repeated again and again to the indifferent van-driver. 'She was here last night, but she did say something about going to her daughter in Manchester.' And off they went to die in the Home.

Hetty knew that when houses have been emptied for redevelopment they may stay empty for months, even years. She intended to go on living in this one until the builders moved in.

It was a warm autumn. For the first time in her life she lived like her gipsy forebears, and did not go to bed in a room in a house like respectable people. She spent several nights, with Tibby, sitting crouched in a doorway of an empty house two doors from her own. She knew exactly when the police would come around, and where to hide herself in the bushes of the overgrown shrubby garden.

As she had expected, nothing happened in the house, and she moved back in. She smashed a back windowpane so that Tibby could move in and out without her having to unlock the front door for him, and without leaving a window

suspiciously open. She moved to the top back room and left
it every morning early, to spend the day in the streets with
her pram and her rags. At night she kept a candle
glimmering low down on the floor. The lavatory was still
out of order, so she used a pail on the first floor instead,
and secretly emptied it at night into the canal which in the
day was full of pleasure boats and people fishing.

Tibby brought her several pigeons during that time.

'Oh, you are a clever puss, Tibby, Tibby! Oh, you're
clever, you are. You know how things are, don't you, you
know how to get around and about.'

The weather turned very cold; Christmas came and
went. Hetty's cough came back, and she spent most of her
time under piles of blankets and old clothes, dozing. At
night she watched the shadows of the candle flame on floor
and ceiling – the window-frames fitted badly, and there
was a daught. Twice tramps spent the night in the bottom
of the house and she heard them being moved on by the
police. She had to go down to make sure the police had not
blocked up the broken window the cat used, but they had
not. A blackbird had flown in and had battered itself to
death trying to get out. She plucked it, and roasted it over
a fire made with bits of floorboard in a baking-pan; the gas
of course had been cut off. She had never eaten very much,
and was not frightened that some dry bread and a bit of
cheese was all that she had eaten during her sojourn under
the heap of clothes. She was cold, but did not think about
that much. Outside there was slushy brown snow everywhere. She went back to her nest, thinking that soon the
cold spell would be over and she could get back to her
trading. Tibby sometimes got into the pile with her, and
she clutched the warmth of him to her. 'Oh, you clever cat,
you clever old thing, looking after yourself, aren't you?
That's right, my ducky, that's right, my lovely.'

And then, just as she was moving about again, with
snow gone off the ground for a time but winter only just
begun, in January, she saw a builder's van draw up
outside, a couple of men unloading their gear. They did not
come into the house: they were to start work next day. By
then Hetty, her cat, her pram piled with clothes and her
two blankets, were gone. She also took a box of matches, a

candle, an old saucepan and a fork and spoon, a tin-opener, a candle and a rat-trap. She had a horror of rats.

About two miles away, among the homes and gardens of amiable Hampstead, where live so many of the rich, the intelligent and the famous, stood three empty, very large houses. She had seen them on an occasion, a couple of years before, when she had taken a bus. This was a rare thing for her, because of the remarks and curious looks provoked by her mad clothes, and by her being able to appear at the same time such a tough battling old thing, and a naughty child. For the older she got, this disreputable tramp, the more there strengthened in her a quality of fierce, demanding childishness. It was all too much of a mixture; she was uncomfortable to have near.

She was afraid that 'they' might have rebuilt the houses, but there they still stood, too tumbledown and dangerous to be of much use to tramps, let alone the armies of London's homeless. There was no glass left anywhere. The flooring at ground level was mostly gone, leaving small platforms and juts of planking over basements full of water. The ceilings were crumbling. The roofs were going. The houses were like bombed buildings.

But in the cold dark of a late afternoon she pulled the pram up the broken stairs and moved cautiously around the frail boards of a second-floor room that had a great hole in it right down to the bottom of the house. Looking into it was like looking into a well. She held a candle to examine the state of the walls, here more or less whole, and saw that rain and wind blowing in from the window would leave one corner dry. Here she made her home. A sycamore tree screened the gaping window from the main road twenty yards away. Tibby, who was cramped after making the journey under the clothes piled in the pram, bounded down and out and vanished into neglected undergrowth to catch his supper. He returned fed and pleased, and seemed happy to stay clutched in her hard thin old arms. She had come to watch for his return after hunting trips, because the warm purring bundle of bones and fur did seem to allay, for a while, the permanent ache of cold in her bones.

Next day she sold her Edwardian boots for a few shil-

lings – they were fashionable again – and bought a loaf
and some bacon scraps. In a corner of the ruins well away
from the one she had made her own, she pulled up some
floorboards, built a fire, and toasted bread and the bacon
scraps. Tibby had brought in a pigeon, and she roasted
that, but not very efficiently. She was afraid of the fire
catching and the whole mass going up in flames; she was
afraid, too, of the smoke showing and attracting the police.
She had to keep damping down the fire, and so the bird
was bloody and unappetizing, and in the end Tibby got
most of it. She felt confused, and discouraged, but thought
it was because of the long stretch of winter still ahead of
her before spring could come. In fact, she was ill. She made
a couple of attempts to trade and earn money to feed
herself before she acknowledged she was ill. She knew she
was not yet dangerously ill, for she had been that in her
life, and would have been able to recognize the cold listless
indifference of a real last-ditch illness. But all her bones
ached, and her head ached, and she coughed more than
she ever had. Yet she still did not think of herself as
suffering particularly from the cold, even in that sleety
January weather. She had never, in all her life, lived in a
properly heated place, had never known a really warm
home, not even when she lived in the Council flats. Those
flats had electric fires, and the family had never used
them, for the sake of the economy, except in very bad spells
of cold. They piled clothes on to themselves, or went to bed
early. But she did know that to keep herself from dying
now she could not treat the cold with her usual indifference. She knew she must eat. In the comparatively dry
corner of the windy room, away from the gaping window
through which snow and sleet were drifting, she made
another nest – her last. She had found a piece of polythene
sheeting in the rubble, and she laid that down first, so that
the damp would not strike up. Then she spread her two
blankets over that. Over them were heaped the mass of old
clothes. She wished she had another piece of polythene to
put on top, but she used sheets of newspaper instead. She
heaved herself into the middle of this, with a loaf of bread
neaer to hand. She dozed, and waited, and nibbled bits of
bread, and watched the snow drifting softly in. Tibby sat

close to the old blue face that poked out of the pile and put
up a paw to touch it. He miaowed and was restless, and
then went out into the frosty morning and brought in a
pigeon. This the cat put, still struggling and fluttering a
little, close to the old woman. But she was afraid to get out
of the pile in which the heat was being made and kept with
such difficulty. She really could not climb out long enough
to pull up more splinters of plank from the floors, to make
a fire, to pluck the pigeon, to roast it. She put out a cold
hand to stroke the cat.

'Tibby, you old thing, you brought it for me, then, did
you? You did, did you? Come here, come in here . . .' But
he did not want to get in with her. He miaowed again,
pushed the bird closer to her. It was now limp and dead.

'You have it, then. You eat it. I'm not hungry, thank you,
Tibby.'

But the carcass did not interest him. He had eaten a
pigeon before bringing this one up to Hetty. He fed himself
well. In spite of his matted fur, and his scars and his half-
closed yellow eye, he was a strong, healthy cat.

At about four the next morning there were steps and
voices downstairs. Hetty shot out of the pile and crouched
behind a fallen heap of plaster and beams, now covered
with snow, at the end of the room near the window. She
could see through the hole in the floorboards down to the
first floor, which had collapsed entirely, and through it to
the ground floor. She saw a man in a thick overcoat and
muffler and leather gloves holding a strong torch to illu-
minate a thin bundle of clothes lying on the floor. She saw
that this bundle was a sleeping man or woman. She was
indignant – *her* home was being trespassed upon. And she
was afraid because she had not been aware of this other
tenant of the ruin. Had he, or she, heard her talking to the
cat? And where was the cat? If he wasn't careful he would
be caught, and that would be the end of him! The man
with a torch went off and came back with a second man.
In the thick dark far below Hetty, was a small cave of
strong light, which was the torchlight. In this space of
light two men bent to lift the bundle, which was the corpse
of a man or a woman like Hetty. They carried it out across
the danger-traps of fallen and rotting boards that made

gangplanks over the water-filled basements. One man was holding the torch in the hand that supported the dead person's feet, and the light jogged and lurched over trees and grasses: the corpse was being taken through the shrubberies to a car.

There are men in London who, between the hours of two and five in the morning, when the real citizens are asleep, who should not be disturbed by such unpleasantness as the corpses of the poor, make the rounds of all the empty, rotting houses they know about, to collect the dead, and to warn the living that they ought not to be there at all, inviting them to one of the official Homes or lodgings for the homeless.

Hetty was too frightened to get back into her warm heap. She sat with the blankets pulled around her, and looked through gaps in the fabric of the house, making out shapes and boundaries and holes and puddles and mounds of rubble, as her eyes, like her cat's, became accustomed to the dark.

She heard scuffling sounds and knew they were rats. She had meant to set the trap, but the thought of her friend Tibby, who might catch his paw, had stopped her. She sat up until the morning light came in grey and cold, after nine. Now she did know herself to be very ill and in danger, for she had lost all the warmth she had huddled into her bones under the rags. She shivered violently. She was shaking herself apart with shivering. In between spasms she drooped limp and exhausted. Through the ceiling above her – but it was not a ceiling, only a cobweb of slats and planks – she could see into a dark cave which had been a garrett, and through the roof above that, the grey sky, teeming with incipient rain. The cat came back from where he had been hiding, and sat crouched on her knees, keeping her stomach warm, while she thought out her position. These were her last clear thoughts. She told herself that she would not last out until spring unless she allowed 'them' to find her, and take her to hospital. After that, she would be taken to a Home.

But what would happen to Tibby, her poor cat? She rubbed the old beast's scruffy head with the ball of her thumb and muttered: 'Tibby, Tibby, they won't get you, no, you'll be all right, yes, I'll look after you.'

Towards midday, the sun oozed yellow through miles of greasy grey cloud, and she staggered down the rotting stairs, to the shops. Even in those London streets, where the extraordinary has become usual, people turned to stare at a tall gaunt woman, with a white face that had flaming red patches on it, and blue compressed lips, and restless black eyes. She wore a tightly buttoned man's overcoat, torn brown woollen mittens, and an old fur hood. She pushed a pram loaded with old dresses and scraps of embroidery and torn jerseys and shoes, all stirred into a tight tangle, and she kept pushing this pram up against people as they stood in queues, or gossiped, or stared into windows, and she muttered: 'Give me your old clothes, darling, give me your old pretties, give Hetty something, poor Hetty's hungry.' A woman gave her a handful of small change, and Hetty bought a roll filled with tomato and lettuce. She did not dare go into a café, for even in her confused state she knew she would offend, and would probably be asked to leave. But she begged a cup of tea at a street stall, and when the hot sweet liquid flooded through her she felt she might survive the winter. She bought a carton of milk and pushed the pram back through the slushy snowy street to the ruins.

Tibby was not there. She urinated down through the hole in the boards, muttering, 'A nuisance, that old tea,' and wrapped herself in a blanket and waited for the dark to come.

Tibby came in later. He had blood on his foreleg. She had heard scuffling and she knew that he had fought a rat, or several, and had been bitten. She poured the milk into the tilted saucepan and Tibby drank it all.

She spent the night with the animal held against her chilly bosom. They did not sleep, but dozed off and on. Tibby would normally be hunting, the night was his time, but he had stayed with the old woman now for three nights.

Early next morning they again heard the corpse-removers among the rubble on the ground floor, and saw the beams of the torch moving on wet walls and collapsed beams. For a moment the torchlight was almost straight on Hetty, but no one came up: who could believe that a person could be desperate enough to climb those dangerous stairs, to trust those crumbling splintery floors, and in the middle of winter?

Hetty had now stopped thinking of herself as ill, of the degrees of her illness, of her danger – of the impossibility of her surviving. She had cancelled out in her mind the presence of winter and its lethal weather, and it was as if spring were nearly here. She knew that if it had been spring when she had had to leave the other house, she and the cat could have lived here for months and months, quite safely and comfortably. Because it seemed to her an impossible and even a silly thing that her life, or, rather, her death, could depend on something so arbitrary as builders starting work on a house in January rather than in April, she could not believe it: the fact would not stay in her mind. The day before she had been quite clear-headed. But today her thoughts were cloudy, and she talked and laughed aloud. Once she scrambled up and rummaged in her rags for an old Christmas card she had got four years before from her good daughter.

In a harsh angry grumbling voice she said to her four children that she needed a room of her own now that she was getting on. 'I've been a good mother to you,' she shouted to them before invisible witnesses – former neighbours, welfare workers, a doctor. 'I never let you want for anything, never! When you were little you always had the best of everything! You can ask anybody, go on, ask them then!'

She was restless and made such a noise that Tibby left her and bounded on to the pram and crouched watching her. He was limping, and his foreleg was rusty with blood. The rat had bitten deep. When the daylight came, he left Hetty in a kind of a sleep, and went down into the garden where he saw a pigeon feeding on the edge of the pavement. The cat pounced on the bird, dragged it into the bushes, and ate it all, without taking it up to his mistress. After he had finished eating, he stayed hidden, watching the passing people. He stared at them intently with his blazing yellow eye, as if he were thinking, or planning. He did not go into the old ruin and up the crumbling wet stairs until late – it was as if he knew it was not worth while going at all.

He found Hetty, apparently asleep, wrapped loosely in a blanket, propped sitting in a corner. Her head had fallen on her chest, and her quantities of white hair had escaped from a scarlet woollen cap, and concealed a face that was flushed a deceptive pink – the flush of coma from cold. She was not yet dead, but she died that night. The rats came up the walls and along the planks and the cat fled down and away from them, limping still, into the bushes.

Hetty was not found for a couple of weeks. The weather changed to warm, and the man whose job it was to look for corpses was led up the dangerous stairs by the smell. There was something left of her, but not much.

As for the cat, he lingered for two or three days in the thick shrubberies, watching the passing people and beyond them, the thundering traffic of the main road. Once a couple stopped to talk on the pavement, and the cat, seeing two pairs of legs, moved out and rubbed himself against one of the legs. A hand came down and he was stroked and patted for a little. Then the people went away.

The cat saw he would not find another home, and he moved off, nosing and feeling his way from one garden to another, through empty houses, finally into an old church-yard. This graveyard already had a couple of stray cats in it, and he joined them. It was the beginning of a community of stray cats going wild. They killed birds, and the field mice that lived among the grasses, and they drank from puddles. Before winter had ended the cats had had a hard time of it from thirst, during the two long spells when the ground froze and there was snow and no puddles and the birds were hard to catch because the cats were so easy to see against the clean white. But on the whole they managed quite well. One of the cats was female, and soon there were a swarm of wild cats, as wild as if they did not live in the middle of a city surrounded by streets and houses. This was just one of half a dozen communities of wild cats living in that square mile of London.

Then an official came to trap the cats and take them away. Some of them escaped, hiding till it was safe to come back again. But Tibby was caught. Not only was he getting old and stiff – he still limped from the rat's bite – but he was friendly, and did not run away from the man, who had only to pick him up in his arms.

'You're an old soldier, aren't you?' said the man. 'A real tough one, a real old tramp.'

It is possible that the cat even thought that he might be finding another human friend and a home.

But it was not so. The haul of wild cats that week numbered hundreds, and while if Tibby had been younger a home might have been found for him, since he was amiable, and wished to be liked by the human race, he was really too old, and smelly and battered. So they gave him an injection and, as we say, 'put him to sleep'.

Alice Walker

Alice Walker is a poet, novelist and essayist. She was born in 1944 in Eatonton, Georgia, USA, the eighth child in a sharecropper's family. A childhood accident left her permanently blind in one eye.

She studied at Spelman College and then Sarah Lawrence College, graduating in 1965. She had been writing seriously since childhood, and whilst at college showed her poems to Muriel Rukeyser, her tutor, who was herself a poet. Rukeyser contacted a publisher, and Walker's first volume of poems, *Once*, was published in 1968. She married in 1967 and divorced in 1976; she has one daughter.

Alice Walker was active in the civil rights movement and has a fierce commitment to equal rights for black people. She teaches Black Studies, has been writer in residence at various colleges and universities, and from 1974 was a contributing editor to *Ms* magazine. She has published several volumes of poems and two books of short stories as well as her novels, and a collection of essays. *The Color Purple*, published in 1982, was the first novel by a black woman to win the prestigious Pulitzer Prize. In 1985, *The Color Purple* was filmed by Steven Spielberg. In recent years Walker has shown an increasing commitment to the environment and the spiritual importance of nature.

'To Hell With Dying' is from her collection *In Love and Trouble* published in the United States in 1973. It has also been produced as an illustrated book in its own right.

To Hell with Dying

Alice Walker

'To hell with dying,' my father would say. 'These children want Mr Sweet!'

Mr Sweet was a diabetic and an alcoholic and a guitar player and lived down the road from us on a neglected cotton farm. My older brothers and sisters got the most benefit from Mr Sweet, for when they were growing up he had quite a few years ahead of him and so was capable of being called back from the brink of death any number of times – whenever the voice of my father reached him as he lay expiring. 'To hell with dying, man,' my father would say, pushing the wife away from the bedside (in tears although she knew the death was not necessarily the last one unless Mr Sweet really wanted it to be). 'These children want Mr Sweet!' And they did want him, for at a signal from Father they would come crowding around the bed and throw themselves on the covers, and whoever was the smallest at the time would kiss him all over his wrinkled brown face and begin to tickle him so that he would laugh all down in his stomach, and his moustache, which was long and sort of straggly, would shake like Spanish moss and was also that color.

Mr Sweet had been ambitious as a boy, wanted to be a doctor or lawyer or sailor, only to find that black men fare better if they are not. Since he could become none of these things he turned to fishing as his only earnest career and playing the guitar as his only claim to doing anything extraordinarily well. His son, the only one that he and his wife, Miss Mary, had, was shiftless as the day is long and spent money as if he were trying to see the bottom of the mint, which Mr Sweet would tell him was the clean brown

palm of his hand. Miss Mary loved her 'baby', however,
and worked hard to get him the 'lil'l necessaries' of life,
which turned out mostly to be women.

Mr Sweet was a tall, thinnish man with thick kinky hair
going dead white. He was dark brown, his eyes were very
squinty and sort of bluish, and he chewed Brown Mule
tobacco. He was constantly on the verge of being blind
drunk, for he brewed his own liquor and was not in the
least a stingy sort of man, and was always very melancholy
and sad, though, frequently when he was 'feelin' good' he'd
dance around the yard with us, usually keeling over just
as my mother came to see what the commotion was.

Toward all of us children he was very kind, and had the
grace to be shy with us, which is unusual in grown-ups.
He had great respect for my mother for she never held his
drunkenness against him and would let us play with him
even when he was about to fall in the fireplace from drink.
Although Mr Sweet would sometimes lose complete or
nearly complete control of his head and neck so that he
would loll in his chair, his mind remained strangely acute
and his speech not too affected. His ability to be drunk and
sober at the same time made him an ideal playmate, for
he was as weak as we were and we could usually best him
in wrestling, all the while keeping a fairly coherent conversation going.

We never felt anything of Mr Sweet's age when we
played with him. We loved his wrinkles and would draw
some on our brows to be like him, and his white hair was
my special treasure and he knew it and would never come
to visit us just after he had had his hair cut off at the
barbershop. Once he came to our house for something,
probably to see my father about fertilizer for his crops
because, although he never paid the slightest attention to
his crops, he liked to know what things would be best to
use on them if he ever did. Anyhow, he had not come with
his hair since he had just had it shaved off at the barbershop. He wore a huge straw hat to keep off the sun and
also to keep his head away from me. But as soon as I saw
him I ran up and demanded that he take me up and kiss
me with his funny beard which smelled so strongly of
tobacco. Looking forward to burying my small fingers into

his woolly hair I threw away his hat only to find he had done something to his hair, that it was no longer there! I let out a squall which made my mother think that Mr Sweet had finally dropped me in the well or something and from that day I've been wary of men in hats. However, not long after, Mr Sweet showed up with his hair grown out and just as white and kinky and impenetrable as it ever was.

Mr Sweet used to call me his princess, and I believed it. He made me feel pretty at five and six, and simply outrageously devastating at the blazing age of eight and a half. When he came to our house with his guitar the whole family would stop whatever they were doing to sit around him and listen to him play. He liked to play 'Sweet Georgia Brown,' that was what he called me sometimes, and also he liked to play 'Caldonia' and all sorts of sweet, sad, wonderful songs which he sometimes made up. It was from one of these songs that I learned that he had had to marry Miss Mary when he had in fact loved somebody else (now living in Chica-go, or Destroy, Michigan). He was not sure that Joe Lee, her 'baby,' was also his baby. Sometimes he would cry and that was an indication that he was about to die again. And so we would all get prepared, for we were sure to be called upon.

I was seven the first time I remember actually participating in one of Mr Sweet's 'revivals' – my parents told me I had participated before, I had been the one chosen to kiss him and tickle him long before I knew the rite of Mr Sweet's rehabilitation. He had come to our house, it was a few years after his wife's death, and was very sad, and also, typically, very drunk. He sat on the floor next to me and my older brother, the rest of the children were grown up and lived elsewhere, and began to play his guitar and cry. I held his woolly head in my arms and wished I could have been old enough to have been the woman he loved so much and that I had not been lost years and years ago.

When he was leaving, my mother said to us that we'd better sleep light that night for we'd probably have to go over to Mr Sweet's before daylight. And we did. For soon after we had gone to bed one of the neighbors knocked on our door and called my father and said that Mr Sweet was sinking fast and if he wanted to get in a word before the crossover he'd better shake a leg and get over to Mr Sweet's house. All the neighbors knew to come to our house if something was wrong with Mr Sweet, but they did not know how we always managed to make him well, or at least stop him from dying, when he was often so near death. As soon as we heard the cry we got up, my brother and I and my mother and father, and put on our clothes. We hurried out of the house and down the road for we were always afraid that we might someday be too late and Mr Sweet would get tired of dallying.

When we got to the house, a very poor shack really, we found the front room full of neighbors and relatives and someone met us at the door and said that it was all very sad that old Mr Sweet Little (for Little was his family name, although we mostly ignored it) was about to kick the bucket. My parents were advised not to take my brother and me into the 'death room,' seeing we were so young and all, but we were so much more accustomed to the death room than he that we ignored him and dashed in without giving his warning a second thought. I was almost in tears, for these deaths upset me fearfully, and the thought of how much depended on me and my brother (who was such a ham most of the time) made me very nervous.

The doctor was bending over the bed and turned back to tell us for at least the tenth time in the history of my family that, alas, old Mr Sweet Little was dying and that the children had best not see the face of implacable death (I didn't know what 'implacable' was, but whatever it was, Mr Sweet was not!). My father pushed him rather abruptly out of the way saying, as he always did and very loudly for he was saying it to Mr Sweet, 'To hell with dying, man, these children want Mr Sweet' – which was my cue to throw myself upon the bed and kiss Mr Sweet all around the whiskers and under the eyes and around the collar of his nightshirt where he smelled so strongly of all sorts of things, mostly liniment.

I was very good at bringing him around, for as soon as I saw that he was struggling to open his eyes I knew he was going to be all right, and so could finish my revival sure of success. As soon as his eyes were open he would begin to smile and that way I knew that I had surely won. Once, though, I got a tremendous scare, for he could not open his eyes and later I learned that he had had a stroke and that one side of his face was stiff and hard to get into motion. When he began to smile I could tickle him in earnest because I was sure that nothing would get in the way of his laughter, although once he began to cough so hard that he almost threw me off his stomach, but that was when I was very small, little more than a baby, and my bushy hair had gotten in his nose.

When we were sure he would listen to us we would ask him why he was in bed and when he was coming to see us again and could we play with his guitar, which more than likely would be leaning against the bed. His eyes would get all misty and he would sometimes cry out loud, but we never let it embarrass us, for he knew that we loved him and that we sometimes cried too for no reason. My parents would leave the room to just the three of us; Mr Sweet, by that time, would be propped up in bed with a number of pillows behind his head and with me sitting and lying on his shoulder and along his chest. Even when he had trouble breathing he would not ask me to get down. Looking into my eyes he would shake his white head and run a scratchy old finger all around my hairline, which was rather low down, nearly to my eyebrows, and made some people say I looked like a baby monkey.

My brother was very generous in all this, he let me do all the revivaling – he had done it for years before I was born and so was glad to be able to pass it on to someone new. What he would do while I talked to Mr Sweet was pretend to play the guitar, in fact pretend that he was a young version of Mr Sweet, and it always made Mr Sweet glad to think that someone wanted to be like him – of course, we did not know this then, we played the thing by ear, and whatever he seemed to like, we did. We were desperately afraid that he was just going to take off one day and leave us.

It did not occur to us that we were doing anything special; we had not learned that death was final when it did come. We thought nothing of triumphing over it so many times, and in fact became a trifle contemptuous of people who let themselves be carried away. It did not occur to us that if our own father had been dying we could not have stopped it, that Mr Sweet was the only person over whom we had power.

When Mr Sweet was in his eighties I was studying in the university many miles from home. I saw him whenever I went home, but he was never on the verge of dying that I could tell and I began to feel that my anxiety for his health and psychological well-being was unnecessary. By this time he not only had a moustache but a long flowing snow-white beard, which I loved and combed and braided for hours. He was very peaceful, fragile, gentle, and the only jarring note about him was his old steel guitar, which he still played in the old sad, sweet, down-home blues way.

On Mr Sweet's ninetieth birthday I was finishing my doctorate in Massachusetts and had been making arrangements to go home for several weeks' rest. That morning I got a telegram telling me that Mr Sweet was dying again and could I please drop everything and come home. Of course I could. My dissertation could wait and my teachers would understand when I explained to them when I got back. I ran to the phone, called the airport, and within four hours I was speeding along the dusty road to Mr Sweet's.

The house was more dilapidated than when I was last there, barely a shack, but it was overgrown with yellow roses which my family had planted many years ago. The air was heavy and sweet and very peaceful. I felt strange walking through the gate and up the old rickety steps. But the strangeness left me as I caught sight of the long white beard I loved so well flowing down the thin body over the familiar quilt coverlet. Mr Sweet!

His eyes were closed tight and his hands, crossed over his stomach, were thin and delicate, no longer scratchy. I remembered how always before I had run and jumped up on him just anywhere; now I knew he would not be able to support my weight. I looked around at my parents, and was surprised to see that my father and mother also looked old and frail. My father, his own hair very gray, leaned over the quietly sleeping old man, who, incidentally, smelled still of wine and tobacco, and said, as he'd done so many times, 'To hell with dying, man! My daughter is home to see Mr Sweet!' My brother had not been able to come as he was in the war in Asia. I bent down and gently stroked the closed eyes and gradually they began to open. The closed, wine-stained lips twitched a little, then parted in a warm, slightly embarrassed smile. Mr Sweet could see me and he recognized me and his eyes looked very spry and twinkly for a moment. I put my head down on the pillow next to his and we just looked at each other for a long time. Then he began to trace my peculiar hairline with a thin, smooth finger. I closed my eyes when his finger halted above my ear (he used to rejoice at the dirt in my ears when I was little), his hand stayed cupped around my cheek. When I opened my eyes, sure that I had reached him in time, his were closed.

Even at twenty-four how could I believe that I had failed? that Mr Sweet was really gone? He had never gone before. But when I looked up at my parents I saw that they were holding back tears. They had loved him dearly. He was like a piece of rare and delicate china which was always being saved from breaking and which finally fell. I looked long at the old face, the wrinkled forehead, the red lips, the hands that still reached out to me. Soon I felt my father pushing something cool into my hands. It was Mr Sweet's guitar. He had asked them months before to give it to me; he had known that even if I came next time he would not be able to respond in the old way. He did not want me to feel that my trip had been for nothing.

The old guitar! I plucked the strings, hummed 'Sweet Georgia Brown.' The magic of Mr Sweet lingered still in the cool steel box. Through the window I could catch the fragrant delicate scent of tender yellow roses. The man on the high old-fashioned bed with the quilt coverlet and the flowing white beard had been my first love.

Sylvia Plath

Sylvia Plath was born in Massachusetts in America in 1932. Her father, who was of German origin, died when she was eight years old; her mother, a teacher of Austrian extraction, encouraged Plath's early interest in writing. Whilst she was at high school and at Smith College in the early 1950s, Plath was successful in getting several of her stories and poems published in magazines.

In 1953 Sylvia Plath suffered a serious nervous breakdown and attempted suicide. She wrote about her experience of schizophrenic and suicidal feelings in a powerful novel, *The Bell Jar*, which was published in 1963. After graduating from college, Sylvia Plath won a Fulbright Scholarship to study in Cambridge, England. There she met and married the poet Ted Hughes. They travelled together to the USA where Plath taught for a year, and returned to England in 1960 when the first book of Plath's poems, *The Colossus*, was published. She gave birth to a daughter in 1960 and a son in 1962.

Her radio play *Three Women: A Monologue for Three Voices*, broadcast in 1962, indicates her fragile state of mind and sense of a divided self. In 1963 Sylvia Plath made a bonfire of some of her own and some of Hughes' manuscripts, took her children from Devon to London, and committed suicide by gassing herself. Her brilliant and bitter poems, many about relationships between men and women, were published in 1965 after her death under the title *Ariel*. The story we have chosen 'The Day Mr Prescott Died', was written in 1956.

The Day Mr Prescott Died
Sylvia Plath

It was a bright day, a hot day, the day old Mr Prescott
died. Mama and I sat on the side seat of the rickety green
bus from the subway station to Devonshire Terrace and
jogged and jogged. The sweat was trickling down my back,
I could feel it, and my black linen was stuck solid against
the seat. Every time I moved it would come loose with a
tearing sound, and I gave Mama an angry 'so there' look,
just like it was her fault, which it wasn't. But she only sat
with her hands folded in her lap, jouncing up and down,
and didn't say anything. Just looked resigned to fate is all.

'I say, Mama,' I'd told her after Mrs Mayfair called that
morning, 'I can see going to the funeral even though I don't
believe in funerals, only what do you mean we have to sit
up and watch with them?'

'It is what you do when somebody close dies,' Mama said,
very reasonable. 'You go over and sit with them. It is a bad
time.'

'So it is a bad time,' I argued. 'So what can I do, not
seeing Liz and Ben Prescott since I was a kid except once
a year at Christmas time for giving presents at Mrs
Mayfair's. I am supposed to sit around hold handkerchiefs,
maybe?'

With that remark, Mama up and slapped me across the
mouth, the way she hadn't done since I was a little kid and
very fresh. 'You are coming with me,' she said in her
dignified tone that means definitely no more fooling.

So that is how I happened to be sitting in this bus on the
hottest day of the year. I wasn't sure how you dressed for
waiting up with people, but I figured as long as it was
black it was all right. So I had on this real smart black
linen suit and a little veil hat, like I wear to the office

when I go out to dinner nights, and I felt ready for anything.

Well, the bus chugged along and we went through the real bad parts of East Boston I hadn't seen since I was a kid. Ever since we moved to the country with Aunt Myra, I hadn't come back to my home town. The only thing I really missed after we moved was the ocean. Even today on this bus I caught myself waiting for that first stretch of blue.

'Look, Mama, there's the old beach,' I said, pointing.

Mama looked and smiled. 'Yes.' Then she turned around to me and her thin face got very serious. 'I want you to make me proud of you today. When you talk, talk. But talk nice. None of this fancy business about burning people up like roast pigs. It isn't decent.'

'Oh, Mama,' I said, very tired. I was always explaining. 'Don't you know I've got better sense. Just because old Mr Prescott had it coming. Just because nobody's sorry, don't think I won't be nice and proper.'

I knew that would get Mama. 'What do you mean nobody's sorry?' she hissed at me, first making sure people weren't near enough to listen. 'What do you mean, talking so nasty?'

'Now, Mama,' I said, 'you know Mr Prescott was twenty years older than Mrs Prescott and she was just waiting for him to die so she could have some fun. Just waiting. He was a grumpy old man even as far back as I remember. A cross word for everybody, and he kept getting that skin disease on his hands.'

'That was a pity the poor man couldn't help,' Mama said piously. 'He had a right to be crotchety over his hands itching all the time, rubbing them the way he did.'

'Remember the time he came to Christmas Eve supper last year?' I went on stubbornly. 'He sat at the table and kept rubbing his hands so loud you couldn't hear anything else, only the skin like sandpaper flaking off in little pieces. How would you like to live with *that* every day?'

I had her there. No doubt about it, Mr Prescott's going was no sorrow for anybody. It was the best thing that could have happened all round.

'Well,' Mama breathed, 'we can at least be glad he went

so quick and easy. I only hope I go like that when my time comes.'

Then the streets were crowding up together all of a sudden, and there we were by old Devonshire Terrace and Mama was pulling the buzzer. The bus dived to a stop, and I grabbed hold of the chipped chromium pole behind the driver just before I would have shot out the front window. 'Thanks, mister,' I said in my best icy tone, and minced down from the bus.

'Remember,' Mama said as we walked down the sidewalk, going single file where there was a hydrant, it was so narrow, 'remember, we stay as long as they need us. And no complaining. Just wash dishes, or talk to Liz, or whatever.'

'But Mama,' I complained, 'how can I say I'm sorry about Mr Prescott when I'm really not sorry at all? When I really think it's a good thing?'

'You can say it is the mercy of the Lord he went so peaceful,' Mama said sternly. 'Then you will be telling the honest truth.'

I got nervous only when we turned up the little gravel drive by the old yellow house the Prescotts owned on Devonshire Terrace. I didn't feel even the least bit sad. The orange-and-green awning was out over the porch, just like I remembered, and after ten years it didn't look any different, only smaller. And the two poplar trees on each side of the door had shrunk, but that was all.

As I helped Mama up the stone steps onto the porch, I could hear a creaking and sure enough, there was Ben Prescott sitting and swinging on the porch hammock like it was any other day in the world but the one his Pop died. He just sat there, lanky and tall as life. What really surprised me was he had his favourite guitar in the hammock beside him. Like he'd just finished playing 'The Big Rock Candy Mountain', or something.

'Hello Ben,' Mama said mournfully. 'I'm so sorry.'

Ben looked embarrassed. 'Heck, that's all right,' he said. 'The folks are all in the living-room.'

I followed Mama in through the screen door, giving Ben a little smile. I didn't know whether it was right to smile because Ben was a nice guy, or whether I shouldn't, out of respect for his Pop.

Inside the house, it was like I remembered too, very dark so you could hardly see, and the green window blinds didn't help. They were all pulled down. Because of the heat or the funeral, I couldn't tell. Mama felt her way to the livingroom and drew back the portieres. 'Lydia?' she called.

'Agnes?' There was this little stir in the dark of the livingroom and Mrs Prescott came out to meet us. I had never seen her looking so well, even though the powder on her face was all streaked from crying.

I only stood there while the two of them hugged and kissed and made sympathetic little noises to each other. Then Mrs Prescott turned to me and gave me her cheek to kiss. I tried to look sad again but it just wouldn't come, so I said, 'You don't know how surprised we were to hear about Mr Prescott.' Really, though, nobody was at all surprised, because the old man only needed one more heart attack and that would be that. But it was the right thing to say.

'Ah, yes,' Mrs Prescott sighed. 'I hadn't thought to see this day for many a long year yet.' And she led us into the living-room.

After I got used to the dim light, I could make out the people sitting around. There was Mrs Mayfair, who was Mrs Prescott's sister-in-law and the most enormous woman I've ever seen. She was in the corner by the piano. Then there was Liz, who barely said hello to me. She was in shorts and an old shirt, smoking one drag after the other. For a girl who had seen her father die that morning, she was real casual, only a little pale is all.

Well, when we were all settled, no one said anything for a minute, as if waiting for a cue, like before a show begins. Only Mrs Mayfair, sitting there in her layers of fat, was wiping away her eyes with a handkerchief, and I was reasonably sure it was sweat running down and not tears by a long shot.

'It's a shame,' Mama began then, very low, 'It's a shame, Lydia, that it had to happen like this. I was so quick in coming I didn't hear tell who found him even.'

Mama pronounced 'him' like it should have a capital H,

but I guessed it was safe now that old Mr Prescott wouldn't
be bothering anybody again, with the mean temper and
those raspy hands. Anyhow, it was just the lead that Mrs
Prescott was waiting for.

'Oh, Agnes,' she began, with a peculiar shining light to
her face, 'I wasn't even here. It was Liz found him, poor
child.'

'Poor child,' sniffed Mrs Mayfair into her handkerchief.
Her huge red face wrinkled up like a cracked watermelon.
'He dropped dead right in her arms, he did.'

Liz didn't say anything, but just ground out one cigarette
only half smoked and lit another. Her hands weren't even
shaking. And believe me, I looked real carefully.

'I was at the rabbi's,' Mrs Prescott took up. She is a great
one for the new religions. All the time it is some new
minister or preacher having dinner at her house. So now
it's a rabbi, yet. 'I was at the rabbi's, and Liz was home
getting dinner when Pop came home from swimming. You
know the way he always loved to swim, Agnes.'

Mama said yes, she knew the way Mr Prescott always
loved to swim.

'Well,' Mrs Prescott went on, calm as this guy on the
Dragnet program, 'it wasn't more than eleven-thirty. Pop
always liked a morning dip, even when the water was like
ice, and he came up and was in the yard drying off, talking
to our next door neighbor over the hollyhock fence.'

'He just put up that very fence a year ago,' Mrs Mayfair
interrupted, like it was an important clue.

'And Mr Gove, this nice man next door, thought Pop
looked funny, blue, he said, and Pop all at once didn't
answer him but just stood there staring with a silly smile
on his face.'

Liz was looking out of the front window where there was
still the sound of the hammock creaking on the front porch.
She was blowing smoke rings. Not a word the whole time.
Smoke rings only.

'So Mr Gove yells to Liz and she comes running out, and
Pop falls like a tree right to the ground, and Mr Gove runs
to get some brandy in the house while Liz holds Pop in her
arms . . .'

'What happened then?' I couldn't help asking, just the

way I used to when I was a kid and Mama was telling burglar stories.

'Then,' Mrs Prescott told us, 'Pop just ... passed away, right there in Liz's arms. Before he could even finish the brandy.'

'Oh, Lydia,' Mama cried. 'What you have been through!'

Mrs Prescott didn't look as if she had been through much of anything. Mrs Mayfair began sobbing in her handkerchief and invoking the name of the Lord. She must have had it in for the old guy, because she kept praying, 'Oh, forgive us our sins,' like she had up and killed him herself.

'We will go on,' Mrs Prescott said, smiling bravely. 'Pop would have wanted us to go on.'

'That is all the best of us can do,' Mama sighed.

'I only hope I go as peacefully,' Mrs Prescott said.

'Forgive us our sins,' Mrs Mayfair sobbed to no one in particular.

At this point, the creaking of the hammock stopped outside and Ben Prescott stood in the doorway, blinking his eyes behind the thick glasses and trying to see where we all were in the dark. 'I'm hungry,' he said.

'I think we should all eat now,' Mrs Prescott smiled on us. 'The neighbors have brought over enough to last a week.'

'Turkey and ham, soup and salad,' Liz remarked in a bored tone, like she was a waitress reading off a menu. 'I just didn't know where to put it all.'

'Oh, Lydia,' Mama exclaimed, 'Let *us* get it ready. Let *us* help. I hope it isn't too much trouble ...'

'Trouble, no,' Mrs Prescott smiled her new radiant smile. 'We'll let the young folks get it.'

Mama turned to me with one of her purposeful nods and I jumped up like I had an electric shock. 'Show me where the things are, Liz,' I said, 'and we'll get this set up in no time.'

Ben tailed us out to the kitchen, where the black old gas stove was, and the sink, full of dirty dishes. First thing I did was pick up a big heavy glass soaking in the sink and run myself a long drink of water.

'My, I'm thirsty,' I said and gulped it down. Liz and Ben were staring at me like they were hypnotized. Then I noticed the water had a funny taste, as if I hadn't washed out the glass well enough and there were drops of some strong drink left in the bottom to mix with the water.

'That,' said Liz after a drag on her cigarette, 'is the last glass Pop drank out of. But never mind.'

'Oh Lordy, I'm sorry,' I said, putting it down fast. All at once I felt very much like being sick because I had a picture of old Mr Prescott, drinking his last from the glass and turning blue. 'I really am sorry.'

Ben grinned. 'Somebody's got to drink out of it someday.' I liked Ben. He was always a practical guy when he wanted to be.

Liz went upstairs to change then, after showing me what to get ready for supper.

'Mind if I bring in my guitar?' Ben asked, while I was starting to fix up the potato salad.

'Sure, it's okay by me,' I said. 'Only won't folks talk? Guitars being mostly for parties and all?'

'So let them talk. I've got a yen to strum.'

I made tracks around the kitchen and Ben didn't say much, only sat and played these hillbilly songs very soft, that made you want to laugh and sometimes cry.

'You know, Ben,' I said, cutting up a plate of cold turkey, 'I wonder, are you really sorry.'

Ben grinned, that way he has. 'Not really sorry, now, but I could have been nicer. Could have been nicer, that's all.'

I thought of Mama, and suddenly all the sad part I hadn't been able to find during the day came up in my throat. 'We'll go on better than before,' I said. And then I quoted Mama like I never thought I would: 'It's all the best of us can do.' And I went to take the hot pea soup off the stove.

'Queer, isn't it,' Ben said. 'How you think something is dead and you're free, and then you find it sitting in your own guts laughing at you. Like I don't feel Papa has really died. He's down there somewhere inside of me, looking at what's going on. And grinning away.'

'That can be the good part,' I said, suddenly knowing that it really could. 'The part you don't have to run from.

You know you take it with you, and then when you go any place, it's not running away. It's just growing up.'

Ben smiled at me, and I went to call the folks in. Supper was kind of a quiet meal, with lots of good cold ham and turkey. We talked about my job at the insurance office, and I even made Mrs Mayfair laugh, telling about my boss Mr Murray and his trick cigars. Liz was almost engaged, Mrs Prescott said, and she wasn't half herself unless Barry was around. Not a mention of old Mr Prescott.

Mrs Mayfair gorged herself on three desserts and kept saying, 'Just a sliver, that's all. Just a sliver!' when the chocolate cake went round.

'Poor Henrietta,' Mrs Prescott said, watching her enormous sister-in-law spooning down ice cream. 'It's that psychosomatic hunger they're always talking about. Makes her eat so.'

After coffee which Liz made on the grinder, so you could smell how good it was, there was an awkward little silence. Mama kept picking up her cup and sipping from it, although I could tell she was really all through. Liz was smoking again, so there was a small cloud of haze around her. Ben was making an airplane glider out of his paper napkin.

'Well,' Mrs Prescott cleared her throat, 'I guess I'll go over to the parlor now with Henrietta. Understand, Agnes, I'm not old-fashioned about this. It said definitely no flowers and no one needs to come. It's only a few of Pop's business associates kind of expect it.'

'I'll come,' said Mama staunchly.

'The children aren't going,' Mrs Prescott said. 'They've had enough already.'

'Barry's coming over later,' Liz said. 'I have to wash up.'

'I will do the dishes,' I volunteered, not looking at Mama. 'Ben will help me.'

'Well, that takes care of everybody, I guess.' Mrs Prescott helped Mrs Mayfair to her feet, and Mama took her other arm. The last I saw of them, they were holding Mrs Mayfair while she backed down the front steps, huffing and puffing. It was the only way she could go down safe, without falling, she said.

Angela Carter

Angela Carter was born in 1940 in Eastbourne, Sussex and educated at Bristol University. She is best known, perhaps, as a writer of fantasy and magic-realist fiction. Her works include: *The Magic Toyshop* (1967), *The Bloody Chamber and Other Stories* (1979), *Nights At The Circus* (1984) and *Wise Children* (1991).

Angela Carter had a lifelong interest in folklore and spent several years collecting English folk songs, she also translated and edited *The Virago Book Of Fairy Tales* volumes 1 and 2 (1990/2). Apart from legends, myths and marvels, Carter also immersed herself in carnival, music hall, pantomime and film. 'I like,' she said just before her early death in 1992, 'anything that flickers.' ·

Her writings reveal a passionate energy often linked with a wild comic flair. Her style, with its emphasis on visual detail and imagery, is often poetic in its intensity.

The story selected here is an original re-working of the traditional story of Cinderella or Aschenputtel (*Cinderfool* in the Grimms' telling of 1812). In Angela Carter's version the absent mother is replaced by a nurturing ghost whose mothering power, as well as her vengefulness, extends beyond the grave.

Ashputtle: or, the Mother's Ghost
Angela Carter

A burned child lived in the ashes. No, not really burned –
more charred, a little bit charred, like a stick half-burned
and picked off the fire; she looked like charcoal and ashes
because she lived in the ashes since her mother died and
the hot ashes burned her, so she was scabbed and scarred.
The burned child lived on the hearth, covered in ashes, as
if she was still mourning.

After her mother died and was buried, her father forgot
the mother and forgot the child and married the woman
who used to rake the ashes, and that was why the child
lived in the unraked ashes and there was nobody to brush
her hair, so it stuck out like a mat, nor to wipe the dirt off
her scabbed face and she had no heart to do it for herself,
but she raked the ashes and slept beside the little cat and
got the burned bits from the bottom of the pot to eat,
scraping them out, squatting on the floor, by herself in
front of the fire, not as if she were human, because she was
still mourning.

Her mother was dead and buried but still felt perfect,
exquisite pain of love when she looked up through the
earth and saw the burned child covered in ashes.

'Milk the cow, burned child, and bring back all the milk,'
said the stepmother, who used to rake the ashes and milk
the cow before, but now the burned child did all that.

The ghost of the mother went into the cow.

'Drink some milk and grow fat,' said the mother's ghost.

The burned child pulled on the udder and drank enough
milk before she took the bucket back and nobody saw and
time passed and she grew fat, she grew breasts, she grew
up.

There was a man the stepmother wanted and she asked

him into the kitchen to give him his dinner, but she let the burned child cook it, although the stepmother did all the cooking before. After the burned child cooked the dinner the stepmother sent her off to milk the cow.

'I want that man for myself,' said the burned child to the cow.

The cow let down more milk, and more, and more, enough for the girl to have a drink and wash her face and wash her hands. When she washed her face, she washed the scabs off and now she was not burned at all, but the cow was empty.

'You must give your own milk, next time,' said the ghost of the mother inside the cow. 'You've milked me dry.'

The little cat came by. The ghost of the mother went into the cat.

'Your hair wants doing,' said the cat. 'Lie down.'

The little cat unpicked her raggy lugs with its clever paws until the burned child's hair hung down nicely, but it had been so snagged and tangled that the cat's claws were all pulled out before it was finished.

'Comb your own hair, next time,' said the cat. 'You've taken my strength away, I can't do it again.'

The burned child was clean and combed but stark naked. There was a bird sitting in the apple tree. The ghost of the mother left the cat and went into the bird. The bird struck its own breast with its beak. Blood poured down onto the burned child under the tree. It ran over her shoulders and covered her front and covered her back. She shouted out when it ran down her legs. When the bird had no more blood, the burned child got a red silk dress.

'Bleed your own dress, next time,' said the bird. 'I'm through with all that.'

The burned child went into the kitchen to show herself to the man. She was not burned any more, but lovely. The man left off looking at the stepmother and looked at the girl.

'Come home with me and let your stepmother stay and rake the ashes,' he said to her and off they went. He gave her a house and money. She did all right for herself.

'Now I can go to sleep,' said the ghost of the mother. 'Now everything is all right.'

Jane Gardam

Jane Gardam was born in Coatham, Yorkshire in 1928. After studying literature at London University she went on to become a journalist and writer. She married David Gardam in 1952 and has two sons and one daughter.

She is well known for her children's writing including *A Long Way From Verona* (1971), *The Summer After The Funeral* (1973) and *Bilgewater* (1976).

The landscape for her stories is often the northeast coast of England, whilst the theme is often the process of growing up. The world in which her characters move is peopled by the mildly eccentric middle-class. The adults are often kind and well-intentioned, but do not notice what is going on around them. It is left to the young people to see clearly and to direct the action. They look at the adult world and decide how they want to live their lives.

The Pangs of Love and Other Stories (1983), from which the title story is taken, received the Katherine Mansfield Award. Jane Gardam takes the fairy tale of *The Little Mermaid* by Hans Christian Andersen and turns it upside down, telling of the exploits of the little mermaid's youngest sister. Described as 'a difficult child of very different temper', this outspoken and unromantic seventh child takes a no-nonsense approach to the handsome prince. She is determined to put his love to the test and to prove how dangerous love can be – particularly for women.

The Pangs of Love

Jane Gardam

It is not generally known that the good little mermaid of Hans Christian Andersen, who died for love of the handsome prince and allowed herself to dissolve in the foam of the ocean, had a younger sister, a difficult child of very different temper.

She was very young when the tragedy occurred, and was only told it later by her five elder sisters and her grandmother, the Sea King's mother with the twelve important oyster shells in her tail. They spent much of their time, all these women, mourning the tragic life of the little mermaid in the Sea King's palace below the waves, and a very dreary place it had become in consequence.

'I don't see what she did it for,' the seventh little mermaid used to say. 'Love for a man – ridiculous,' and all the others would sway on the tide and moan, 'Hush, hush – you don't know how she suffered for love.'

'I don't understand this "suffered for love,"' said the seventh mermaid. 'She sounds very silly and obviously spoiled her life.'

'She may have spoiled her life,' said the Sea King's mother, 'but think how good she was. She was given the chance of saving her life, but because it would have harmed the prince and his earthly bride she let herself die.'

'What had he done so special to deserve that?' asked the seventh mermaid.

'He had *done* nothing. He was just her beloved prince to whom she would sacrifice all.'

'What did he sacrifice for her?' asked Signorina Settima.

'Not a lot,' said the Sea King's mother, 'I believe they don't on the whole. But it doesn't stop us loving them.'

'It would me,' said the seventh mermaid. 'I must get a

look at some of this mankind, and perhaps I will then understand more.'

'You must wait until your fifteenth birthday,' said the Sea King's mother. 'That has always been the rule with all your sisters.'

'Oh, shit,' said the seventh mermaid (she was rather coarse). 'Times change. I'm as mature now as they were at fifteen. Howsabout tomorrow?'

'I'm sure I don't know what's to be done with you,' said the Sea King's mother, whose character had weakened in later years. 'You are totally different from the others and yet I'm sure I brought you all up the same.'

'Oh no you didn't,' said the five elder sisters in chorus, 'she's always been spoiled. We'd never have dared talk to you like that. Think if our beloved sister who died for love had talked to you like that.'

'Maybe she should have done,' said the dreadful seventh damsel officiously, and this time in spite of her grandmother's failing powers she was put in a cave for a while in the dark and made to miss her supper.

Nevertheless, she was the sort of girl who didn't let other people's views interfere with her too much, and she could argue like nobody else in the sea, so that in the end her grandmother said, 'Oh for goodness' sake then – go. Go now and don't even wait for your *fourteenth* birthday. Go and look at some men and don't come back unless they can turn you into a mermaid one hundredth part as good as your beloved foamy sister.'

'Whoops,' said Mademoiselle Sept, and she flicked her tail and was away up out of the Sea King's palace, rising through the coral and the fishes that wove about the red and blue seaweed trees like birds, up and up until her head shot out into the air and she took a deep breath of it and said, 'Wow!'

The sky, as her admirable sister had noticed, stood above the sea like a large glass bell, and the waves rolled and lifted and tossed towards a green shore where there were fields and palaces and flowers and forests where fish with wings and legs wove about the branches of green and so forth trees, singing at the tops of their voices. On a balcony sticking out from the best palace stood, as he had stood

before his marriage when the immaculate sister had first
seen him, the wonderful prince with his chin resting on his
hand as it often did of an evening – and indeed in the
mornings and afternoons, too.

'Oh help!' said the seventh mermaid, feeling a queer
twisting around the heart. Then she thought, 'Watch it.'
She dived under water for a time and came up on a rock
on the shore, where she sat and examined her sea-green
finger nails and smoothed down the silver scales of her
tail.

She was sitting where the prince could see her and after
a while he gave a cry and she looked up. 'Oh,' he said, 'how
you remind me of someone. I thought for a moment you
were my lost love.'

'Lost love,' said the seventh mermaid. 'And whose fault
was that? She was my sister. She died for love of you and
you never gave her one serious thought. You even took her
along on your honeymoon like a pet toy. I don't know what
she saw in you.'

'I always loved her,' said the prince. 'But I didn't realise
it until too late.'

'That's what they all say,' said Numera Septima. 'Are
you a poet? They're the worst. Hardy, Tennyson, Shakespeare, Homer. Homer was the worst of all. And he hadn't
a good word to say for mermaids.'

'Forgive me,' said the prince, who had removed his chin
from his hand and was passionately clenching the parapet.
'Every word you speak reminds me more and more –'

'I don't see how it can,' said the s.m., 'since for love of
you and because she was told it was the only way she could
come to you, she let them cut out her tongue, the silly ass.'

'And your face,' he cried, 'your whole aspect, except of
course for the tail.'

'She had that removed, too. They told her it would be
agony and it was, so my sisters tell me. It shrivelled up
and she got two ugly stumps called legs – I dare say you've
got them under that parapet. When she danced, every step
she took was like knives.'

'Alas, alas!'

'Catch me getting rid of my tail,' said syedmaya krasav-
itsa, twitching it seductively about, and the prince gave a

great sprint from the balcony and embraced her on the rocks. It was all right until half way down but the scales were cold and prickly. Slimy too, and he shuddered.

'How dare you shudder,' cried La Septième. 'Go back to your earthly bride.'

'She's not here at present,' said the p., 'she's gone to her mother for the weekend. Won't you come in? We can have dinner in the bath.'

The seventh little mermaid spent the whole weekend with the prince in the bath, and he became quite frantic with desire by Monday morning because of the insurmountable problem below the mermaid's waist. 'Your eyes, your hair,' he cried, 'but that's about all.'

'My sister did away with her beautiful tail for love of you,' said the s.m., reading a volume of Descartes over the prince's shoulder as he lay on her sea-green bosom. 'They tell me she even wore a disgusting harness on the top half of her for you, and make-up and dresses. She was the saint of mermaids.'

'Ah, a saint,' said the prince. 'But without your wit, your spark. I would do anything in the world for you.'

'So what about getting rid of your legs?'

'Getting rid of my *legs*?'

'Then you can come and live with me below the waves. No one has legs down there and there's nothing wrong with any of us. As a matter of fact, aesthetically we're a very good species.'

'Get rid of my *legs*?'

'Yes – my grandmother, the Sea King's mother, and the Sea Witch behind the last whirlpool who fixed up my poor sister, silly cow, could see to it for you.'

'Oh, how I love your racy talk,' said the prince. 'It's like nothing I ever heard before. I should love you even with my eyes shut. Even at a distance. Even on the telephone.'

'No fear,' said the seventh m., 'I know all about this waiting by the telephone. All my sisters do it. It never rings when they want it to. It has days and days of terrible silence and they all roll about weeping and chewing their handkerchieves. You don't catch me getting in that condition.'

'Gosh, you're marvellous,' said the prince, who had been to an old-fashioned school, 'I'll do anything –'

'The legs?'

'Hum. Ha. Well – the legs.'

'Carry me back to the rocks,' said the seventh little mermaid, 'I'll leave you to think about it. What's more I hear a disturbance in the hall which heralds the return of your wife. By the way, it wasn't your wife, you know, who saved you from drowning when you got ship-wrecked on your sixteenth birthday. It was my dear old sister once again. "She swam among the spars and planks which drifted on the sea, quite forgetting they might crush her. Then she ducked beneath the water, and rising again on the billows managed at last to reach you who by now" (being fairly feeble in the muscles I'd guess, with all the stately living) "was scarcely able to swim any longer in the raging sea. Your arms, your legs" (ha!) "began to fail you and your beautiful eyes were closed and you must surely have died if my sister had not come to your assistance. She held your head above the water and let the billows drive her and you together wherever they pleased."

'What antique phraseology.'

'It's a translation from the Danish. Anyway, "when the sun rose red and beaming from the water, your cheeks regained the hue of life but your eyes remained closed. My sister kissed –"

('No!')

'" – your lofty handsome brow and stroked back your wet locks ... She kissed you again and longed that you might live." What's more if you'd only woken up then she could have spoken to you. It was when she got obsessed by you back down under the waves again that she went in for all this tongue and tail stuff with the Sea Witch.'

'She was an awfully nice girl,' said the prince, and tears came into his eyes – which was more than they ever could do for a mermaid however sad, because as we know from H. C. Andersen, mermaids can never cry which makes it harder for them.

'The woman I saw when I came to on the beach,' said the prince, 'was she who is now my wife. A good sort of woman but she drinks.'

'I'm not surprised,' said the seventh mermaid. 'I'd drink if I was married to someone who just stood gazing out to sea thinking of a girl he had allowed to turn into foam,' and she flicked her tail and disappeared.

'Now then,' she thought, 'what's to do next?' She was not to go back, her grandmother had said, until she was one hundredth part as good as the little m. her dead sister, now a spirit of air, and although she was a tearaway and, as I say, rather coarse, she was not altogether untouched by the discipline of the Sea King's mother and her upbringing. Yet she could not say that she exactly yearned for her father's palace with all her melancholy sisters singing dreary stuff about the past. Nor was she too thrilled to return to the heaviness of water with all the featherless fishes swimming through the amber windows and butting in to her, and the living flowers growing out of the palace walls like dry rot. However, after flicking about for a bit, once coming up to do an inspection of a fishing boat in difficulties with the tide and enjoying the usual drop-jawed faces, she took a header home into the front room and sat down quietly in a corner.

'You're back,' said the Sea King's mother. 'How was it? I take it you now feel you are a hundredth part as good as your sainted sister?'

'I've always tried to be good,' said the s.m., 'I've just tried to be rationally good and not romantically good, that's all.'

'Now don't start again. I take it you have seen some men?'

'I saw the prince.'

At this the five elder sisters set up a wavering lament.

'Did you feel for him – '

'Oh, feelings, feelings,' said the seventh and rational mermaid, 'I'm sick to death of feelings. He's good looking, I'll give you that, and rather sweet-natured and he's having a rough time at home, but he's totally self-centred. I agree that my sister must have been a true sea-saint to listen to him dripping on about himself all day. He's warm-hearted though, and not at all bad in the bath.'

The Sea King's mother fainted away at this outspoken and uninhibited statement, and the five senior mermaids fled in shock. The seventh mermaid tidied her hair and set off to find the terrible cave of the Sea Witch behind the last whirlpool, briskly pushing aside the disgusting polypi, half plant, half animal, and the fingery seaweeds that had so terrified her dead sister on a similar journey.

'Aha,' said the Sea Witch, stirring a pot of filthy black bouillabaisse, 'you, like your sister, cannot do without me. I suppose you also want to risk body and soul for the human prince up there on the dry earth?'

'Good afternoon, no,' said the seventh mermaid. 'Might I sit down?' (For even the seventh mermaid was polite to the Sea Witch.) 'I want to ask you if, when the prince follows me down here below the waves, you could arrange for him to live with me until the end of time?'

'He'd have to lose his legs. What would he think of that?'

'I think he might consider it. In due course.'

'He would have to learn to sing and not care about clothes or money or possessions or power – what would he think of that?'

'Difficult, but not impossible.'

'He'd have to face the fact that if you fell in love with one of your own kind and married him he would die and also lose his soul as your sister did when he wouldn't make an honest woman of her.'

'It was not,' said the seventh mermaid, 'that he wouldn't make an honest woman of her. It just never occurred to him. After all – she couldn't speak to him about it. You had cut out her tongue.'

'Aha,' said the s.w., 'it's different for a man, is it? Falling in love, are you?'

'Certainly not,' said Fräulein Sieben. 'Certainly not.'

'Cruel then, eh? Revengeful? Or do you hate men? It's very fashionable.'

'I'm not cruel. Or revengeful. I'm just rational. And I don't hate men. I think I'd probably like them very much, especially if they are all as kind and as beautiful as the prince. I just don't believe in falling in love with them. It is a burden and it spoils life. It is a mental illness. It killed my sister and it puts women in a weak position and makes us to be considered second class.'

'They fall in love with us,' said the Sea Witch. 'That's to say, with women. So I've been told. Sometimes. Haven't you read the sonnets of Shakespeare and the poems of Petrarch?'

'The sonnets of Shakespeare are hardly all about one woman,' said the bright young mermaid. 'In fact some of them are written to a man. As for Petrarch, (there was scarcely a thing this girl hadn't read) he only saw his girl once, walking over a bridge. They never exactly brushed their teeth together.'

'Well, there are the Brownings.'

'Yes. The Brownings were all right,' said the mermaid. 'Very funny looking though. I don't suppose anyone else ever wanted them.'

'You are a determined young mermaid,' said the Sea Witch. 'Yes, I'll agree to treat the prince if he comes this way. But you must wait and see if he does.'

'Thank you, yes I will,' said the seventh mermaid. 'He'll come,' and she did wait, quite confidently, being the kind of girl well-heeled men do run after because she never ran after them, very like Elizabeth Bennet.

So, one day, who should come swimming down through the wonderful blue water and into the golden palaces of the Sea King and floating through the windows like the fish and touching with wonder the dry-rot flowers upon the walls, but the prince, his golden hair floating behind him and his golden hose and tunic stuck tight to him all over like a wet-suit, and he looked terrific.

'Oh, princess, sweet seventh mermaid,' he said, finding her at once (because she was the sort of girl who is always in the right place at the right time). 'I have found you again. Ever since I threw you back in the sea I have dreamed of you. I cannot live without you. I have left my boozy wife and have come to live with you for ever.'

'There are terrible conditions,' said the seventh mermaid. 'Remember. The same conditions which my poor sister accepted in reverse. You must lose your legs and wear a tail.

'This I will do.'

'You must learn to sing for hours and hours in unison with the other mermen, in wondrous notes that hypnotise simple sailors up above and make them think they hear faint sounds from Glyndebourne or Milan.'

'As to that,' said the prince, 'I always wished I had a voice.'

'And you must know that if I decide that I want someone more than you, someone of my own sort, and marry him, you will lose everything, as my sister did – your body, your immortal soul and your self-respect.'

'Oh well, that's quite all right,' said the prince. He knew that no girl could ever prefer anyone else to him.

'*Right*,' said the mermaid. 'Well, before we go off to the Sea Witch, let's give a party. And let me introduce you to my mother and sisters.'

Then there followed a time of most glorious celebration similar only to the celebration some years back for the prince's wedding night when the poor little mermaid now dead had had to sit on the deck of the nuptial barque and watch the bride and groom until she had quite melted away. Then the cannons had roared and the flags had waved and a royal bridal tent of cloth of gold and purple and precious furs had been set upon the deck and when it grew dark, coloured lamps had been lit and sailors danced merrily and the bride and groom had gone into the tent without the prince giving the little mermaid a backward glance.

Now, beneath the waves the sea was similarly alight with glowing corals and brilliant sea-flowers and a bower was set up for the seventh mermaid and the prince and she danced with all the mermen who had silver crowns on their heads and St Christophers round their necks, very trendy like the South of France, and they all had a lovely time.

And the party went on and on. It was beautiful. Day after day and night after night and anyone who was anyone was there, and the weather was gorgeous – no storms below or above and it was exactly as Hans Christian Andersen said: 'a wondrous blue tint lay over everything; one would be more inclined to fancy one was high up in the air and saw nothing but sky above and below than that one was at the bottom of the sea. During a calm, too, one could catch a glimpse of the sun. It looked like a crimson flower from the cup of which, light streamed forth.' The seventh mermaid danced and danced, particularly with a handsome young merman with whom she seemed much at her ease.

'Who is that merman?' asked the prince. 'You seem to know him well.'

'Oh – just an old friend,' said the seventh m., 'he's always been about. We were in our prams together.' (This was not true. The seventh m. was just testing the prince. She had never bothered with mermen even in her pram.)

'I'm sorry,' said the prince, 'I can't have you having mermen friends. Even if there's nothing in it.'

'We must discuss this with the Sea Witch,' said the seventh mermaid, and taking his hand she swam with him out of the palace and away and away through the dreadful polypi again. She took him past the last whirlpool to the cave where the Sea Witch was sitting eating a most unpleasant-looking type of caviar from a giant snail shell and stroking her necklace of sea snakes.

'Ha,' said the Sea Witch, 'the prince. You have come to be rid of your legs?'

'Er – well –'

'You have come to be rid of your earthly speech, your clothes and possessions and power?'

'Well, it's something that we might discuss.'

'And you agree to lose soul and body and self-respect if this interesting mermaid goes off and marries someone?'

There was a very long silence and the seventh mermaid closely examined some shells round her neck, tiny pale pink oyster shells each containing a pearl which would be the glory of a Queen's crown. The prince held his beautiful chin in his lovely, sensitive hand. His gentle eyes filled with tears. At last he took the mermaid's small hand and kissed its palm and folded the sea-green nails over the kiss (he had sweet ways) and said, 'I must not look at you. I must go at once,' and he pushed off. That is to say, he pushed himself upwards off the floor of the sea and shot up and away and away through the foam, arriving home in time for tea and early sherry with his wife, who was much relieved.

It was a very long time indeed before the seventh little mermaid returned to the party. In fact the party was all but over. There was only the odd slithery merman twanging a harp of dead fisherman's bones and the greediest and grubbiest of the deep water fishes eating up the last of the sandwiches. The Sea King's old mother was asleep, her heavy tail studded with important oyster shells coiled round the legs of her throne.

The five elder sisters had gone on somewhere amusing.

The seventh mermaid sat down at the feet of her grandmother and at length the old lady woke up and surveyed the chaos left over from the fun. 'Hullo, my child,' she said. 'Are you alone?'

'Yes. The prince has gone. The engagement's off.'

'My dear – what did I tell you? Remember how your poor sister suffered. I warned you.'

'Pooh – I'm not suffering. I've just proved my point. Men aren't worth it.'

'Maybe you and she were unfortunate,' said the Sea King's mother. 'Which men you meet is very much a matter of luck, I'm told.'

'No – they're all the same,' said the mermaid who by now was nearly fifteen years old. 'I've proved what I suspected. I'm free now – free of the terrible pangs of love which put women in bondage, and I shall dedicate my life to freeing and instructing other women and saving them from humiliation.'

'Well, I hope you don't become one of those frowsty little women who don't laugh and have only one subject of conversation,' said the Sea Witch. 'It is a mistake to base a whole philosophy upon one disappointment.'

'Disappointment – pah!' said the seventh mermaid. 'When was I ever negative?'

'And I hope you don't become aggressive.'

'When was I ever aggressive?' said Senorita Septima ferociously.

'That's a good girl then,' said the Sea King's mother, 'So now – unclench that fist.'

Tillie Olsen

Tillie Olsen was born in Omaha, Nebraska, USA in 1913. She is the daughter of working class parents who fled from Russia after the failed revolution of 1905. Times were hard for the family. Tille Olsen left school early to earn money to contribute to the family income, continuing her education by reading widely from the public libraries.

Olsen's father was secretary of the Nebraska Socialist Party, and throughout her life, Olsen has had an active commitment to politics. At seventeen she joined the Young Communist League. In 1932 she was jailed for handing out pamphlets to packing house workers. From 1936 she lived with Jack Olsen, a printer and union man who became her husband in 1943.

Olsen was nineteen when she wrote her first novel *Yonnondio* (a native American word meaning 'lament for the lost'). During the period when she was bringing up her four daughters, her family and political commitments left her no time to write. She started writing again in the late 1950s, and a collection of her short stories *Tell Me A Riddle* was published in 1961. A talk she had given in 1962 on the silences in her own and other women writers' careers was presented in book form, *Silences*, in 1965. Since then she has written, taught and edited women's fiction, and been writer in residence at different American universities. In 1984 she published a collection of women's writing on the theme of mother and daughter relationships, *Mother to Daughter, Daughter to Mother*. This same theme appears in the story 'I Stand Here Ironing' which is from the collection *Tell Me A Riddle*.

I Stand Here Ironing
Tillie Olsen

I stand here ironing, and what you asked me moves tormented back and forth with the iron.

'I wish you would manage the time to come in and talk with me about your daughter. I'm sure you can help me understand her. She's a youngster who needs help and whom I'm deeply interested in helping.'

'Who needs help . . .' Even if I came, what good would it do? You think because I am her mother I have a key, or that in some way you could use me as a key? She has lived for nineteen years. There is all that life that has happened outside of me, beyond me.

And when is there time to remember, to sift, to weigh, to estimate, to total? I will start and there will be an interruption and I will have to gather it all together again. Or I will become engulfed with all I did or did not do, with what should have been and what cannot be helped.

She was a beautiful baby. The first and only one of our five that was beautiful at birth. You do not guess how new and uneasy her tenancy in her now-loveliness. You did not know her all those years she was thought homely, or see her poring over her baby pictures, making me tell her over and over how beautiful she had been – and would be, I would tell her – and was now, to the seeing eye. But the seeing eyes were few or non-existent. Including mine.

I nursed her. They feel that's important nowadays. I nursed all the children, but with her, with all the fierce rigidity of first motherhood, I did like the books then said. Though her cries battered me to trembling and my breasts ached with swollenness, I waited till the clock decreed.

Why do I put that first? I do not even know if it matters, or if it explains anything.

She was a beautiful baby. She blew shining bubbles of sound. She loved motion, loved light, loved colour and music and textures. She would lie on the floor in her blue overalls patting the surface so hard in ecstasy her hands and feet would blur. She was a miracle to me, but when she was eight months old I had to leave her daytimes with the woman downstairs to whom she was no miracle at all, for I worked or looked for work and for Emily's father, who 'could no longer endure' (he wrote in his good-bye note) 'sharing want with us.'

I was nineteen. It was the pre-relief, pre-WPA world of the depression. I would start running as soon as I got off the streetcar, running up the stairs, the place smelling sour, and awake or asleep to startle awake, when she saw me she would break into a clogged weeping that could not be comforted, a weeping I can yet hear.

After a while I found a job hashing at night so I could be with her days, and it was better. But it came to where I had to bring her to his family and leave her.

It took a long time to raise the money for her fare back. Then she got chicken pox and I had to wait longer. When she finally came, I hardly knew her, walking quick and nervous like her father, looking like her father, thin, and dressed in a shoddy red that yellowed her skin and glared at the pock marks. All the baby loveliness gone.

She was two. Old enough for nursery school they said, and I did not know then what I know now – the fatigue of the long day, and the lacerations of group life in the kinds of nurseries that are only parking places for children.

Except that it would have made no difference if I had known. It was the only place there was. It was the only way we could be together, the only way I could hold a job.

And even without knowing, I knew. I knew the teacher that was evil because all these years it has curdled into my memory, the little boy hunched in the corner, her rasp, 'why aren't you outside, because Alvin hits you? that's no reason, go out, scaredy.' I knew Emily hated it even if she did not clutch and implore 'don't go Mommy' like the other children, mornings.

She always had a reason why we should stay home. Momma, you look sick. Momma, I feel sick. Momma, the teachers aren't there today, they're sick. Momma, we can't go, there was a fire there last night. Momma, it's a holiday today, no school, they told me.

But never a direct protest, never rebellion. I think of our others in their three-, four-year-oldness – the explosions, the tempers, the denunciations, the demands – and I feel suddenly ill. I put the iron down. What in me demanded that goodness in her? And what was the cost, the cost to her of such goodness?

The old man living in the back once said in his gentle way: 'You should smile at Emily more when you look at her.' What *was* in my face when I looked at her? I loved her. There were all the acts of love.

It was only with the others I remembered what he said, and it was the face of joy, and not of care or tightness or worry I turned to them – too late for Emily. She does not smile easily, let alone almost always as her brothers and sisters do. Her face is closed and sombre, but when she wants, how fluid. You must have seen it in her panto-mimes, you spoke of her rare gift for comedy on the stage that rouses a laughter out of the audience so dear they applaud and applaud and do not want to let her go.

Where does it come from, that comedy? There was none of it in her when she came back to me that second time, after I had had to send her away again. She had a new daddy now to learn to love, and I think perhaps it was a better time. Except when we left her alone nights, telling ourselves she was old enough.

'Can't you go some other time, Mommy, like tomorrow?' she would ask. 'Will it be just a little while you'll be gone? Do you promise?'

The time we came back, the front door open, the clock on the floor in the hall. She rigid awake. 'It wasn't just a little while. I didn't cry. Three times I called you, just three times, and then I ran downstairs to open the door so you could come faster. The clock talked loud. I threw it away, it scared me what it talked.'

She said the clock talked loud again that night I went to the hospital to have Susan. She was delirious with the fever that comes before red measles, but she was fully conscious all the week I was gone and the week after we

were home when she could not come near the new baby or
me.

She did not get well. She stayed skeleton thin, not
wanting to eat, and night after night she had nightmares.
She would call for me, and I would rouse from exhaustion
to sleepily call back: 'You're all right, darling, go to sleep,
it's just a dream,' and if she still called, in a sterner voice,
'now go to sleep, Emily, there's nothing to hurt you.' Twice,
only twice, when I had to get up for Susan anyhow, I went
in to sit with her.

Now when it is too late (as if she would let me hold and
comfort her like I do the others) I get up and go to her at
once at her moan or restless stirring. 'Are you awake,
Emily? Can I get you something, dear?' And the answer is
always the same: 'No, I'm all right, go back to sleep,
Mother.'

They persuaded me at the clinic to send her away to a
convalescent home in the country where 'she can have the
kind of food and care you can't manage for her, and you'll
be free to concentrate on the new baby.' They still send
children to that place. I see pictures on the society page of
sleek young women planning affairs to raise money for it,
or dancing at the affairs, or decorating Easter eggs or
filling Christmas stockings for the children.

They never have a picture of the children so I do not
know if the girls still wear those gigantic red bows and the
ravaged looks on the every other Sunday when parents
can come to visit 'unless otherwise notified' – as we were
notified the first six weeks.

Oh it is a handsome place, green lawns and tall trees
and fluted flower beds. High up on the balconies of each
cottage the children stand, the girls in their red bows and
white dresses, the boys in white suits and giant red ties.
The parents stand below shrieking up to be heard and the
children shriek down to be heard, and between them the
invisible wall 'Not To Be Contaminated by Parental Germs
or Physical Affection.'

There was a tiny girl who always stood hand in hand
with Emily. Her parents never came. One visit she was
gone. 'They moved her to Rose Cottage,' Emily shouted in
explanation. 'They don't like you to love anybody here.'

She wrote once a week, the laboured writing of a seven-year-old. 'I am fine. How is the baby. If I write my leter nicly I will have a star. Love.' There never was a star. We wrote every other day, letters she could never hold or keep but only hear read – once. 'We simply do not have room for children to keep any personal possessions,' they patiently explained when we pieced one Sunday's shrieking together to plead how much it would mean to Emily, who loved so to keep things, to be allowed to keep her letters and cards.

Each visit she looked frailer. 'She isn't eating,' they told us.

(They had runny eggs for breakfast or mush with lumps, Emily said later, I'd hold it in my mouth and not swallow. Nothing ever tasted good, just when they had chicken.)

It took us eight months to get her released home, and only the fact that she gained back so little of her seven lost pounds convinced the social worker.

I used to try to hold and love her after she came back, but her body would stay stiff, and after a while she'd push away. She ate little. Food sickened her, and I think much of life too. Oh she had physical lightness and brightness, twinkling by on skates, bouncing like a ball up and down up and down over the jump rope, skimming over the hill; but these were momentary.

She fretted about her appearance, thin and dark and foreign-looking at a time when every little girl was supposed to look or thought she should look a chubby blonde replica of Shirley Temple. The door-bell sometimes rang for her, but no one seemed to come and play in the house or be a best friend. Maybe because we moved so much.

There was a boy she loved painfully through two school semesters. Months later she told me how she had taken pennies from my purse to buy him candy. 'Liquorice was his favourite and I brought him some every day, but he still liked Jennifer better'n me. Why, Mommy?' The kind of question for which there is no answer.

School was a worry to her. She was not glib or quick in a world where glibness and quickness were easily confused with ability to learn. To her overworked and exasperated teachers she was an overconscientious 'slow learner' who kept trying to catch up and was absent entirely too often.

I let her be absent, though sometimes the illness was imaginary. How different from my now-strictness about attendance with the others. I wasn't working. We had a new baby, I was home anyhow. Sometimes, after Susan grew old enough, I would keep her home from school, too, to have them all together.

Mostly Emily had asthma, and her breathing, harsh and laboured, would fill the house with a curiously tranquil sound. I would bring the two old dresser mirrors and her boxes of collections to her bed. She would select beads and single ear-rings, bottle tops and shells, dried flowers and pebbles, old postcards and scraps, all sorts of oddments; then she and Susan would play Kingdom, setting up landscapes and furniture, peopling them with action.

Those were the only times of peaceful companionship between her and Susan. I have edged away from it, that poisonous feeling between them, that terrible balancing of hurts and needs I had to do between the two, and did so badly, those earlier years.

Oh there are conflicts between the others too, each one human, needing, demanding, hurting, taking – but only between Emily and Susan, no, Emily toward Susan that corroding resentment. It seems so obvious on the surface, yet it is not obvious. Susan, the second child, Susan, golden- and curly-haired and chubby, quick and articulate and assured, everything in appearance and manner Emily was not; Susan, not able to resist Emily's precious things, losing or sometimes clumsily breaking them; Susan telling jokes and riddles to company for applause while Emily sat silent (to say to me later: that was *my* riddle, Mother, I told it to Susan); Susan, who for all the five years' difference in age was just a year behind Emily in developing physically.

I am glad for that slow physical development that widened the difference between her and her contemporaries, though she suffered over it. She was too vulnerable for that terrible world of youthful competition, of preening and parading, of constant measuring of yourself against every other, of envy, 'If I had that copper hair,' or 'If I had that skin ...' She tormented herself enough about not looking like the others, there was enough of the unsureness, the having to be conscious of words before you speak, the constant caring – what are they thinking of me? What kind of an impression am I making? – there was enough without having it all magnified by the merciless physical drives.

Ronnie is calling. He is wet and I change him. It is rare there is such a cry now. That time of motherhood is almost behind me when the ear is not one's own but must always be racked and listening for the child cry, the child call. We sit for a while and I hold him, looking out over the city spread in charcoal with its soft aisles of white. '*Shoogily,*' he breathes and curls closer. I carry him back to bed, asleep. *Shoogily*. A funny word, a family word, inherited from Emily, invented by her to say: *comfort.*

In this and other ways she leaves her seal, I say aloud. And startle at my saying it. What do I mean? What did I start to gather together, to try and make coherent? I was at the terrible, growing years. War years. I do not remember them well. I was working, there were four smaller ones now, there was not time for her. She had to help be a mother, and housekeeper, and shopper. She had to set her seal. Mornings of crisis and near hysteria trying to get lunches packed, hair combed, coats and shoes found, everyone to school or Child Care on time, the baby ready for transportation. And always the paper scribbled on by a smaller one, the book looked at by Susan then mislaid, the homework not done. Running out to that huge school where she was one, she was lost, she was a drop; suffering over the unpreparedness, stammering and unsure in her classes.

There was so little time left at night after the kids were bedded down. She would struggle over books, always eating (it was in those years she developed her enormous appetite that is legendary in our family) and I would be ironing, or preparing food for the next day, or writing V-mail to Bill, or tending the baby. Sometimes, to make me laugh, or out of her despair, she would imitate happenings or types at school.

I think I said once: 'Why don't you do something like this in the school amateur show?' One morning she phoned me at work, hardly understandable through the weeping:

'Mother, I did it, I won, I won; they gave me first prize; they clapped and clapped and wouldn't let me go.'

Now suddenly she was Somebody, and as imprisoned in her difference as she had been in anonymity.

She began to be asked to perform at other high schools, even in colleges, then at city and state-wide affairs. The first one we went to, I only recognized her that first moment when thin, shy, she almost drowned herself into the curtains. Then: Was this Emily? The control, the command, the convulsing and deadly clowning, the spell, then the roaring, stamping audience, unwilling to let this rare and precious laughter out of their lives.

Afterwards: You ought to do something about her with a gift like that – but without money or knowing how, what does one do? We have left it all to her, and the gift has as often eddied inside, clogged and clotted, as been used and growing.

She is coming. She runs up the stairs two at a time with her light graceful step, and I know she is happy tonight. Whatever it was that occasioned your call did not happen today.

'Aren't you ever going to finish the ironing, Mother? Whistler painted his mother in a rocker. I'd have to paint mine standing over an ironing-board.' This is one of her communicative nights and she tells me everything and nothing as she fixes herself a plate of food out of the icebox.

She is so lovely. Why did you want me to come in at all? Why were you concerned? She will find her way.

She starts up the stairs to bed. 'Don't get me up with the rest in the morning.' 'But I thought you were having midterms.' 'Oh, those,' she comes back in, kisses me, and says quite lightly, 'in a couple of years when we'll all be atom-dead they won't matter a bit.'

She has said it before. She *believes* it. But because I have been dredging the past, and all that compounds a human being is so heavy and meaningful in me, I cannot endure it tonight.

I will never total it all. I will never come in to say: She was a child seldom smiled at. Her father left me before she was a year old. I had to work her first six years when there was work, or I sent her home and to his relatives. There were years she had care she hated. She was dark and thin and foreign-looking in a world where the prestige went to blondeness and curly hair and dimples, she was slow where glibness was prized. She was a child of anxious, not proud, love. We were poor and could not afford for her the soil of easy growth. I was a young mother, I was a distracted mother. There were the other children pushing up, demanding. Her younger sister seemed all that she was not. There were years she did not let me touch her. She kept too much in herself, her life was such that she had to keep too much in herself. My wisdom came too late. She has much to her and probably little will come of it. She is a child of her age, of depression, of war, of fear.

Let her be. So all that is in her will not bloom – but in how many does it? There is still enough left to live by. Only help her to know – help make it so there is cause for her to know that she is more than this dress on the ironing-board, helpless before the iron.

1953–1954

Margaret Atwood

Margaret Atwood was born in Ottawa, Ontario, Canada in 1939. Much of her early life was spent in the Quebec north bush where her father carried out insect research. The whole family would leave the city for six or seven months at a time, meaning that Margaret Atwood did not attend a full year of school until the eighth grade. Her mother taught her at home and from an early age Margaret Atwood began writing, producing her first collection of poetry *Rhyming Cats* when she was five. She went on to study English Language and Literature at the University of Toronto and then took a Master's degree at Harvard University in the United States, although at that time women were not allowed access to the Lamont library where all the leading modern poetry was kept. Undeterred, or perhaps fired, by such constraints Margaret Atwood has gone on to become one of Canada's leading writers, writing poetry, fiction and critical writing.

She describes herself as a procrastinator, putting off wrtiting until she has reached the deadline. 'Blank pages inspire me with terror. What will I put on them? Will it be good enough? Will I have to throw it out?' Despite such anxieties, Margaret Atwood has produced a fascinating body of work, which has been widely translated. Her novels include *Bodily Harm* (1981), a quasi political thriller, and *Cat's Eye* (1988), which looks at the secrecies and cruelties of childhood. *The Handmaid's Tale* (1985), a futuristic fantasy where women are denied virtually all rights, has been made into a film.

The story 'The Age of Lead' is taken from the short story collection *Wilderness Tips* (1991). The influence of those early years in the Canadian bush are evident in Margaret Atwood's fascination with metamorphosis and the wilderness. A television report on the discovery of a corpse frozen in the Arctic ice for 150 years prompts the viewer, Jane, to reflect on her own life and the death of a friend.

The Age of Lead

Margaret Atwood

The man has been buried for a hundred and fifty years. They dug a hole in the frozen gravel, deep into the permafrost, and put him down there so the wolves couldn't get to him. Or that is the speculation.

When they dug the hole the permafrost was exposed to the air, which was warmer. This made the permafrost melt. But it froze again after the man was covered up, so that when he was brought to the surface he was completely enclosed in ice. They took the lid off the coffin and it was like those maraschino cherries you used to freeze in ice-cube trays for fancy tropical drinks: a vague shape, looming through a solid cloud.

Then they melted the ice and he came to light. He is almost the same as when he was buried. The freezing water has pushed his lips away from his teeth into an astonished snarl, and he's a beige colour, like a gravy stain on linen, instead of pink, but everything is still there. He even has eyeballs, except that they aren't white but the light brown of milky tea. With these tea-stained eyes he regards Jane: an indecipherable gaze, innocent, ferocious, amazed, but contemplative, like a werewolf meditating, caught in a flash of lightning at the exact split second of his tumultuous change.

Jane doesn't watch very much television. She used to watch it more. She used to watch comedy series, in the evenings, and when she was a student at university she would watch afternoon soaps about hospitals and rich people, as a way of procrastinating. For a while, not so long ago, she would watch the evening news, taking in the disasters with her feet tucked up on the chesterfield, a throw rug over her legs, drinking hot milk and rum to relax before bed. It was all a form of escape.

But what you can see on the television, at whatever time of day, is edging too close to her own life; though in her life, nothing stays put in those tidy compartments, comedy here, seedy romance and sentimental tears there, accidents and violent deaths in thirty-second clips they call *bites*, as if they were chocolate bars. In her life, everything is mixed together. *Laugh, I thought I'd die*, Vincent used to say, a very long time ago, in a voice imitating the banality of mothers; and that's how it's getting to be. So when she flicks on the television these days, she flicks it off again soon enough. Even the commercials, with their surreal dailiness, are beginning to look sinister, to suggest meanings behind themselves, behind their façade of cleanliness, lusciousness, health, power, and speed.

Tonight she leaves the television on, because what she is seeing is so unlike what she usually sees. There is nothing sinister behind this image of the frozen man. It is entirely itself. *What you sees is what you gets*, as Vincent also used to say, crossing his eyes, baring his teeth at one side, pushing his nose into a horror-movie snout. Although it never was, with him.

The man they've dug up and melted was a young man. Or still is: it's difficult to know what tense should be applied to him, he is so insistently present. Despite the distortions caused by the ice and the emaciation of his illness, you can see his youthfulness, the absence of toughening, of wear. According to the dates painted carefully onto his nameplate, he was only twenty years old. His name was John Torrington. He was, or is, a sailor, a seaman. He wasn't an able-bodied seaman though; he was a petty officer, one of those marginally in command. Being in command has little to do with the ableness of the body.

He was one of the first to die. This is why he got a coffin and a metal nameplate, and a deep hole in the permafrost – because they still had the energy, and the piety, for such things, that early. There would have been a burial service read over him, and prayers. As time went on and became nebulous and things did not get better, they must have

kept the energy for themselves; and also the prayers. The
prayers would have ceased to be routine and become
desperate, and then hopeless. The later dead ones got
cairns of piled stones, and the much later ones not even
that. They ended up as bones, and as the soles of boots and
the occasional button, sprinkled over the frozen stony
treeless relentless ground in a trail heading south. It was
like the trails in fairy tales, of bread crumbs or seeds or
white stones. But in this case nothing had sprouted or lit
up in the moonlight, forming a miraculous pathway to life;
no rescuers had followed. It took ten years before anyone
knew even the barest beginnings of what had been happen-
ing to them.

All of them together were the Franklin Expedition. Jane
has seldom paid much attention to history except when it
has overlapped with her knowledge of antique furniture
and real estate – '19th C. pine harvest table,' or 'Prime
location Georgian centre hall, impeccable reno' – but she
knows what the Franklin Expedition was. The two ships
with their bad-luck names have been on stamps – the
Terror, the *Erebus*. Also she took it in school, along with a
lot of other doomed expeditions. Not many of those explor-
ers seemed to have come out of it very well. They were
always getting scurvy, or lost.
    What the Franklin Expedition was looking for was the
Northwest Passage, an open seaway across the top of the
Arctic, so people, merchants, could get to India from
England without going all the way around South America.
They wanted to go that way because it would cost less and
increase their profits. This was much less exotic than
Marco Polo or the headwaters of the Nile; nevertheless,
the idea of exploration appealed to her then: to get onto a
boat and just go somewhere, somewhere mapless, off into
the unknown. To launch yourself into fright; to find things
out. There was something daring and noble about it,
despite all of the losses and failures, or perhaps because of
them. It was like having sex, in high school, in those days
before the Pill, even if you took precautions. If you were a
girl, that is. If you were a boy, for whom such a risk was
fairly minimal, you had to do other things: things with

weapons or large amounts of alcohol, or high-speed vehicles, which at her suburban Toronto high school, back then at the beginning of the sixties, meant switchblades, beer, and drag races down the main streets on Saturday nights.

Now, gazing at the television as the lozenge of ice gradually melts and the outline of the young sailor's body clears and sharpens, Jane remembers Vincent, sixteen and with more hair then, quirking one eyebrow and lifting his lip in a mock sneer and saying, 'Franklin, my dear, I don't give a damn.' He said it loud enough to be heard, but the history teacher ignored him, not knowing what else to do. It was hard for the teachers to keep Vincent in line, because he never seemed to be afraid of anything that might happen to him.

He was hollow-eyed even then; he frequently looked as if he'd been up all night. Even then he resembled a very young old man, or else a dissipated child. The dark circles under his eyes were the ancient part, but when he smiled he had lovely small white teeth, like the magazine ads for baby foods. He made fun of everything, and was adored. He wasn't adored the way other boys were adored, those boys with surly lower lips and greased hair and a studied air of smouldering menace. He was adored like a pet. Not a dog, but a cat. He went where he liked, and nobody owned him. Nobody called him Vince.

Strangely enough, Jane's mother approved of him. She didn't usually approve of the boys Jane went out with. Maybe she approved of him because it was obvious to her that no bad results would follow from Jane's going out with him: no heartaches, no heaviness, nothing burdensome. None of what she called *consequences*. Consequences: the weightiness of the body, the growing flesh hauled around like a bundle, the tiny frill-framed goblin head in the carriage. Babies and marriage, in that order. This was how she understood men and their furtive, fumbling, threatening desires, because Jane herself had been a consequence. She had been a mistake, she had been a war baby. She had been a crime that had needed to be paid for, over and over.

By the time she was sixteen, Jane had heard enough about this to last her several lifetimes. In her mother's account of the way things were, you were young briefly and then you fell. You plummeted downwards like an overripe apple and hit the ground with a squash; you fell, and everything about you fell too. You got fallen arches and a fallen womb, and your hair and teeth fell out. That's what having a baby did to you. It subjected you to the force of gravity.

This is how she remembers her mother, still: in terms of a pendulous, drooping, wilting motion. Her sagging breasts, the downturned lines around her mouth. Jane conjures her up: there she is, as usual, sitting at the kitchen table with a cup of cooling tea, exhausted after her job clerking at Eaton's department store, standing all day behind the jewellery counter with her bum stuffed into a girdle and her swelling feet crammed into the mandatory medium-heeled shoes, smiling her envious, disapproving smile at the spoiled customers who turned up their noses at pieces of glittering junk she herself could never afford to buy. Jane's mother sighs, picks up the canned spaghetti Jane has heated up for her. Silent words waft out of her like stale talcum powder: *What can you expect*, always a statement, never a question. Jane tries at this distance for pity, but comes up with none.

As for Jane's father, he'd run away from home when Jane was five, leaving her mother in the lurch. That's what her mother called it – 'running away from home' – as if he'd been an irresponsible child. Money arrived from time to time, but that was the sum total of his contribution to family life. Jane resented him for it, but she didn't blame him. Her mother inspired in almost everyone who encountered her a vicious desire for escape.

Jane and Vincent would sit out in the cramped backyard of Jane's house, which was one of the squinty-windowed little stuccoed wartime bungalows at the bottom of the hill. At the top of the hill were the richer houses, and the richer people: the girls who owned cashmere sweaters, at least one of them, instead of the Orlon and lambswool so familiar to Jane. Vincent lived about halfway up the hill. He still had a father, in theory.

They would sit against the back fence, near the spindly

cosmos flowers that passed for a garden, as far away from the house itself as they could get. They would drink gin, decanted by Vincent from his father's liquor hoard and smuggled in an old military pocket flask he'd picked up somewhere. They would imitate their mothers.

'I pinch and scrape and I work my fingers to the bone, and what thanks do I get?' Vincent would say peevishly. 'No help from you, Sonny Boy. You're just like your father. Free as the birds, out all night, do as you like and you don't care one pin about anyone else's feelings. Now take out that garbage.'

'It's love that does it to you,' Jane would reply, in the resigned, ponderous voice of her mother. 'You wait and see, my girl. One of these days you'll come down off your devil-may-care high horse.' As Jane said this, and even though she was making fun, she could picture love, with a capital L, descending out of the sky towards her like a huge foot. Her mother's life had been a disaster, but in her own view an inevitable disaster, as in songs and movies. It was Love that was responsible, and in the face of Love, what could be done? Love was like a steamroller. There was no avoiding it, it went over you and you came out flat.

Jane's mother waited, fearfully and uttering warnings, but with a sort of gloating relish, for the same thing to happen to Jane. Every time Jane went out with a new boy her mother inspected him as a potential agent of downfall. She distrusted most of these boys; she distrusted their sulky, pulpy mouths, their eyes half-closed in the up-drifting smoke of their cigarettes, their slow, sauntering manner of walking, their clothing that was too tight, too full: too full of their bodies. They looked this way even when they weren't putting on the sulks and swaggers, when they were trying to appear bright-eyed and indus-trious and polite for Jane's mother's benefit, saying good-bye at the front door, dressed in their shirts and ties and their pressed heavy-date suits. They couldn't help the way they looked, the way they were. They were helpless; one kiss in a dark corner would reduce them to speechlessness; they were sleepwalkers in their own liquid bodies. Jane, on the other hand, was wide awake.

Jane and Vincent did not exactly go out together. Instead

they made fun of going out. When the coast was clear and Jane's mother's wasn't home, Vincent would appear at the door with his face painted bright yellow, and Jane would put her bathrobe on back to front and they would order Chinese food and alarm the delivery boy and eat sitting cross-legged on the floor, clumsily, with chopsticks. Or Vincent would turn up in a threadbare thirty-year-old suit and a bowler hat and a cane, and Jane would rummage around in the cupboard for a discarded church-going hat of her mother's, with smashed cloth violets and a veil, and they would go downtown and walk around, making loud remarks about the passers-by, pretending to be old, or poor, or crazy. It was thoughtless and in bad taste, which was what they both liked about it.

Vincent took Jane to the graduation formal, and they picked out her dress together at one of the second-hand clothing shops Vincent frequented, giggling at the shock and admiration they hoped to cause. They hesitated between a flame-red with falling-off sequins and a backless hip-hugging black with a plunge front, and chose the black, to go with Jane's hair. Vincent sent a poisonous-looking lime-green orchid, the colour of her eyes, he said, and Jane painted her eyelids and fingernails to match. Vincent wore white tie and tails, and a top hat, all frayed Sally-Ann issue and ludicrously too large for him. They tangoed around the gymnasium, even though the music was not a tango, under the tissue-paper flowers, cutting a black swathe through the sea of pastel tulle, unsmiling, projecting a corny sexual menace, Vincent with Jane's long pearl necklace clenched between his teeth.

The applause was mostly for him, because of the way he was adored. Though mostly by the girls, thinks Jane. But he seemed to be popular enough among the boys as well. Probably he told them dirty jokes, in the proverbial locker room. He knew enough of them.

As he dipped Jane backwards, he dropped the pearls and whispered into her ear, 'No belts, no pins, no pads, no chafing.' It was from an ad for tampons, but it was also their leitmotif. It was what they both wanted: freedom from the world of mothers, the world of precautions, the world of burdens and fate and heavy female constraints upon the flesh. They wanted a life without consequences. Until recently, they'd managed it.

The scientists have melted the entire length of the young sailor now, at least the upper layer of him. They've been pouring warm water over him, gently and patiently; they don't want to thaw him too abruptly. It's as if John Torrington is asleep and they don't want to startle him.

Now his feet have been revealed. They're bare, and white rather than beige; they look like the feet of someone who's been walking on a cold floor, on a winter day. That is the quality of the light that they reflect: winter sunlight, in early morning. There is something intensely painful to Jane about the absence of socks. They could have left him his socks. But maybe the others needed them. His big toes are tied together with a strip of cloth; the man talking says this was to keep the body tidily packaged for burial, but Jane is not convinced. His arms are tied to his body, his ankles are tied together. You do that when you don't want a person walking around.

This part is almost too much for Jane; it is too reminiscent. She reaches for the channel switcher, but luckily the show (it is only a show, it's only another show) changes to two of the historical experts, analyzing the clothing. There's a close-up of John Torrington's shirt, a simple, high-collared, pin-striped white-and-blue cotton, with mother-of-pearl buttons. The stripes are a printed pattern, rather than a woven one; woven would have been more expensive. The trousers are grey linen. Ah, thinks Jane. Wardrobe. She feels better: this is something she knows about. She loves the solemnity, the reverence, with which the stripes and buttons are discussed. An interest in the clothing of the present is frivolity, an interest in the clothing of the past is archaeology; a point Vincent would have appreciated.

After high school, Jane and Vincent both got scholarships to university, although Vincent had appeared to study less, and did better. That summer they did everything together. They got summer jobs at the same hamburger heaven, they went to movies together after work, although Vincent never paid for Jane. They still occasion-

ally dressed up in old clothes and pretended to be a weird
couple, but it no longer felt careless and filled with absurd
invention. It was beginning to occur to them that they
might conceivably end up looking like that.

In the first year at university Jane stopped going out
with other boys: she needed a part-time job to help pay her
way, and that and the schoolwork and Vincent took up all
her time. She thought she might be in love with Vincent.
She thought that maybe they should make love, to find
out. She had never done such a thing, entirely; she had
been too afraid of the untrustworthiness of men, of the
gravity of love, too afraid of consequences. She thought,
however, that she might trust Vincent.

But things didn't go that way. They held hands, but they
didn't hug; they hugged, but they didn't pet; they kissed,
but they didn't neck. Vincent liked looking at her, but he
liked it so much he would never close his eyes. She would
close hers and then open them, and there would be Vincent, his own eyes shining in the light from the streetlamp
or the moon, peering at her inquisitively as if waiting to
see what odd female thing she would do next, for his
delighted amusement. Making love with Vincent did not
seem altogether possible.

(Later, after she had flung herself into the current of
opinion that had swollen to a river by the late sixties, she
no longer said 'making love'; she said 'having sex.' But it
amounted to the same thing. You had sex, and love got
made out of it whether you liked it or not. You woke up in
a bed or more likely on a mattress, with an arm around
you, and found yourself wondering what it might be like
to keep on doing it. At that point Jane would start looking at her watch. She had no intention of being left in
any lurches. She would do the leaving herself. And she
did.)

Jane and Vincent wandered off to different cities. They
wrote each other postcards. Jane did this and that. She
ran a co-op food store in Vancouver, did the financial stuff
for a diminutive theatre in Montreal, acted as managing
editor for a small publisher, ran the publicity for a dance
company. She had a head for details and for adding up
small sums – having to scrape her way through university

had been instructive – and such jobs were often available if you didn't demand much money for doing them. Jane could see no reason to tie herself down, to make any sort of soul-stunting commitment, to anything or anyone. It was the early seventies; the old heavy women's world of girdles and precautions and consequences had been swept away. There were a lot of windows opening, a lot of doors: you could look in, then you could go in, then you could come out again.

She lived with several men, but in each of the apartments there were always cardboard boxes, belonging to her that she never got around to unpacking; just as well, because it was that much easier to move out. When she got past thirty she decided it might be nice to have a child, sometime, later. She tried to figure out a way of doing this without becoming a mother. Her own mother had moved to Florida, and sent rambling, grumbling letters, to which Jane did not often reply.

Jane moved back to Toronto, and found it ten times more interesting than when she'd left it. Vincent was already there. He'd come back from Europe, where he'd been studying film; he'd opened a design studio. He and Jane met for lunch, and it was the same: the same air of conspiracy between them, the same sense of their own potential for outrageousness. They might still have been sitting in Jane's garden, beside the cosmos flowers, drinking forbidden gin and making fun.

Jane found herself moving in Vincent's circles, or were they orbits? Vincent knew a great many people, people of all kinds; some were artists and some wanted to be, and some wanted to know the ones who were. Some had money to begin with, some made money; they all spent it. There was a lot more talk about money, these days, or among these people. Few of them knew how to manage it, and Jane found herself helping them out. She developed a small business among them, handling their money. She would gather it in, put away safely for them, tell them what they could spend, dole out an allowance. She would note with interest the things they bought, filing their receipted bills: what furniture, what clothing, which *objets*. They were delighted with their money, enchanted with it.

It was like milk and cookies for them, after school. Watching them play with their money, Jane felt responsible and indulgent, and a little matronly. She stored her own money carefully away, and eventually bought a townhouse with it.

All this time she was with Vincent, more or less. They'd tried being lovers but had not made a success of it. Vincent had gone along with this scheme because Jane had wanted it, but he was elusive, he would not make declarations. What worked with other men did not work with him: appeals to his protective instincts, pretences at jealousy, requests to remove stuck lids from jars. Sex with him was more like a musical workout. He couldn't take it seriously, and accused her of being too solemn about it. She thought he might be gay, but was afraid to ask him; she dreaded feeling irrelevant to him, excluded. It took them months to get back to normal.

He was older now, they both were. He had thinning temples and a widow's peak, and his bright inquisitive eyes had receded even further into his head. What went on between them continued to look like a courtship, but was not one. He was always bringing her things: a new, peculiar food to eat, a new grotesquerie to see, a new piece of gossip, which he would present to her with a sense of occasion, like a flower. She in her turn appreciated him. It was like a yogic exericse, appreciating Vincent; it was like appreciating an anchovy, or a stone. He was not everyone's taste.

There's a black-and-white print on the television, then another: the nineteenth century's version of itself, in etchings. Sir John Franklin, older and fatter than Jane had supposed; the *Terror* and the *Erebus*, locked fast in the crush of the ice. In the high Arctic, a hundred and fifty years ago, it's the dead of winter. There is no sun at all, no moon; only the rustling northern lights, like electronic music, and the hard little stars.

What did they do for love, on such a ship, at such a time? Furtive solitary gropings, confused and mournful dreams, the sublimation of novels. The usual, among those who have become solitary.

Down in the hold, surrounded by the creaking of the wooden hull and the stale odours of men far too long enclosed, John Torrington lies dying. He must have known it; you can see it on his face. He turns towards Jane his tea-coloured look of puzzled reproach.

Who held his hand, who read to him, who brought him water? Who, if anyone, loved him? And what did they tell him about whatever it was that was killing him? Consumption, brain fever, Original Sin. All those Victorian reasons, which meant nothing and were the wrong ones. But they must have been comforting. If you are dying, you want to know why.

In the eighties, things started to slide. Toronto was not so much fun any more. There were too many people, too many poor people. You could see them begging on the streets, which were clogged with fumes and cars. The cheap artists' studios were torn down or converted to coy and upscale office space; the artists had migrated elsewhere. Whole streets were torn up or knocked down. The air was full of windblown grit.

People were dying. They were dying too early. One of Jane's clients, a man who owned an antique store, died almost overnight of bone cancer. Another, a woman who was an entertainment lawyer, was trying on a dress in a boutique and had a heart attack. She fell over and they called the ambulance, and she was dead on arrival. A theatrical producer died of aids, and a photographer; the lover of the photographer shot himself, either out of grief or because he knew he was next. A friend of a friend died of emphysema, another of viral pneumonia, another of hepatitis picked up on a tropical vacation, another of spinal meningitis. It was as if they had been weakened by some mysterious agent, a thing like a colourless gas, scentless and invisible, so that any germ that happened along could invade their bodies, take them over.

Jane began to notice news items of the kind she'd once skimmed over. Maple groves dying of acid rain, hormones in the beef, mercury in the fish, pesticides in the vegetables, poison sprayed on the fruit, God knows what in the drinking water. She subscribed to a bottled spring-water service and felt better for a few weeks, then read in the paper that it wouldn't do her much good, because whatever it was had been seeping into everything. Each time you took a breath you breathed some of it in. She thought about moving out of the city, then read about toxic dumps, radioactive waste, concealed here and there in the countryside and masked by the lush, deceitful green of waving trees.

Vincent has been dead for less than a year. He was not put into the permafrost or frozen in ice. He went into the Necropolis, the only Toronto cemetery of whose general ambience he approved; he got flower bulbs planted on top of him, by Jane and others. Mostly by Jane. Right now John Torrington, recently thawed after a hundred and fifty years, probably looks better than Vincent.

A week before Vincent's forty-third birthday, Jane went to see him in the hospital. He was in for tests. Like fun he was. He was in for the unspeakable, the unknown. He was in for a mutated virus that didn't even have a name yet. It was creeping up his spine, and when it reached his brain it would kill him. It was not, as they said, responding to treatment. He was in for the duration.

It was white in his room, wintry. He lay packed in ice, for the pain. A white sheet wrapped him, his white thin feet poked out the bottom of it. They were so pale and cold. Jane took one look at him, laid out on ice like a salmon, and began to cry.

'Oh Vincent,' she said. 'What will I do without you?' This sounded awful. It sounded like Jane and Vincent making fun, of obsolete books, obsolete movies, their obsolete mothers. It also sounded selfish: here she was, worrying about herself and her future, when Vincent was the one who was sick. But it was true. There would be a lot less to do, altogether, without Vincent.

Vincent gazed up at her; the shadows under his eyes were cavernous. 'Lighten up,' he said, not very loudly, because he could not speak very loudly now. By this time she was sitting down, leaning forward; she was holding one of his hands. It was thin as the claw of a bird. 'Who says I'm going to die?' He spent a moment considering this, revised it. 'You're right,' he said. 'They got me. It was the Pod People from outer space. They said, 'All I want is your poddy.''

Jane cried more. It was worse because he was trying to be funny. 'But what *is* it?' she said. 'Have they found out yet?'

Vincent smiled his ancient, jaunty smile, his smile of detachment, of amusement. There were his beautiful teeth, juvenile as ever. 'Who knows?' he said. 'It must have been something I ate.'

Jane sat with the tears running down her face. She felt desolate: left behind, stranded. Their mothers had finally caught up to them and been proven right. There were consequences after all; but they were the consequences to things you didn't even know you'd done.

The scientists are back on the screen. They are excited, their earnest mouths are twitching, you could almost call them joyful. They know why John Torrington died; they know, at last, why the Franklin Expedition went so terribly wrong. They've snipped off pieces of John Torrington, a fingernail, a lock of hair, they've run them through machines and come out with the answers.

There is a shot of an old tin can, pulled open to show the seam. It looks like a bomb casing. A finger points: it was the tin cans that did it, a new invention back then, a new technology, the ultimate defence against starvation and scurvy. The Franklin Expedition was excellently provisioned with tin cans, stuffed full of meat and soup and soldered together with lead. The whole expedition got lead-poisoning. Nobody knew it. Nobody could taste it. It invaded their bones, their lungs, their brains, weakening them and confusing their thinking, so that at the end those that had not yet died in the ships set out in an idiotic trek across the stony, icy ground, pulling a lifeboat laden down with toothbrushes, soap, handkerchiefs, and slippers, useless pieces of junk. When they were found ten years later, they were skeletons in tattered coats, lying where they'd collapsed. They'd been heading back towards the ships. It was what they'd been eating that had killed them.

* * *

Jane switches off the television and goes into her kitchen – all white, done over the year before last, the outmoded butcher-block counters from the seventies torn out and carted away – to make herself some hot milk and rum. Then she decides against it; she won't sleep anyway. Everything in here looks ownerless. Her toaster oven, so perfect for solo dining, her microwave for the vegetables, her espresso maker – they're sitting around waiting for her departure, for this evening or forever, in order to assume their final, real appearances of purposeless objects adrift in the physical world. They might as well be pieces of an exploded spaceship orbiting the moon.

She thinks about Vincent's apartment, so carefully arranged, filled with the beautiful or deliberately ugly possessions he once loved. She thinks about his closet, with its quirky particular outfits, empty now of his arms and legs. It has all been broken up now, sold, given away.

Increasingly the sidewalk that runs past her house is cluttered with plastic drinking cups, crumpled soft-drink cans, used take-out plates. She pick them up, clears them away, but they appear again overnight, like a trail left by an army on the march or by the fleeing residents of a city under bombardment, discarding the objects that were once thought essential but are now too heavy to carry.

Founding Editors: Anne and Ian Serraillier

Chinua Achebe Things Fall Apart
Douglas Adams The Hitchhiker's Guide to the Galaxy
Vivien Alcock The Cuckoo Sister; The Monster Garden; The Trial of Anna Cotman; A Kind of Thief
Margaret Atwood The Handmaid's Tale
J G Ballard Empire of the Sun
Nina Bawden The Witch's Daughter; A Handful of Thieves; Carrie's War; The Robbers; Devil by the Sea; Kept in the Dark; The Finding; Keeping Henry; Humbug
E R Braithwaite To Sir, With Love
John Branfield The Day I Shot My Dad
F Hodgson Burnett The Secret Garden
Ray Bradbury The Golden Apples of the Sun; The Illustrated Man
Betsy Byars The Midnight Fox; Goodbye, Chicken Little; The Pinballs
Victor Canning The Runaways; Flight of the Grey Goose
Ann Coburn Welcome to the Real World
Hannah Cole Bring in the Spring
Jane Leslie Conly Racso and the Rats of NIMH
Robert Cormier We All Fall Down
Roald Dahl Danny, The Champion of the World; The Wonderful Story of Henry Sugar; George's Marvellous Medicine; The BFG; The Witches; Boy; Going Solo; Charlie and the Chocolate Factory; Matilda
Anita Desai The Village by the Sea
Charles Dickens A Christmas Carol; Great Expectations
Peter Dickinson The Gift; Annerton Pit; Healer
Berlie Doherty Granny was a Buffer Girl
Gerald Durrell My Family and Other Animals
J M Falkner Moonfleet
Anne Fine The Granny Project
Anne Frank The Diary of Anne Frank
Leon Garfield Six Apprentices
Jamila Gavin The Wheel of Surya
Adele Geras Snapshots of Paradise

Graham Greene The Third Man and The Fallen Idol; Brighton Rock

Thomas Hardy The Withered Arm and Other Wessex Tales

Rosemary Harris Zed

L P Hartley The Go-Between

Ernest Hemingway The Old Man and the Sea; A Farewell to Arms

Nat Hentoff Does this School have Capital Punishment?

Nigel Hinton Getting Free; Buddy; Buddy's Song

Minfong Ho Rice Without Rain

Anne Holm I Am David

Janni Howker Badger on the Barge; Isaac Campion

Linda Hoy Your Friend Rebecca

Barbara Ireson (Editor) In a Class of Their Own

Jennifer Johnston Shadows on Our Skin

Toeckey Jones Go Well, Stay Well

James Joyce A Portrait of the Artist as a Young Man

Geraldine Kaye Comfort Herself; A Breath of Fresh Air

Clive King Me and My Million

Dick King-Smith The Sheep-Pig

Daniel Keyes Flowers for Algernon

Elizabeth Laird Red Sky in the Morning; Kiss the Dust

D H Lawrence The Fox and The Virgin and the Gypsy; Selected Tales

Harper Lee To Kill a Mockingbird

Julius Lester Basketball Game

Ursula Le Guin A Wizard of Earthsea

C Day Lewis The Otterbury Incident

David Line Run for Your Life; Screaming High

Joan Lingard Across the Barricades; Into Exile; The Clearance; The File on Fraulein Berg

Penelope Lively The Ghost of Thomas Kempe

Jack London The Call of the Wild; White Fang

Bernard Mac Laverty Cal; The Best of Bernard Mac Laverty

Margaret Mahy The Haunting; The Catalogue of The Universe

Jan Mark Do You Read Me? Eight Short Stories

James Vance Marshall Walkabout

Somerset Maugham The Kite and Other Stories

Michael Morpurgo Waiting for Anya; My Friend Walter; The War of Jenkins' Ear

— How many have you read? —